FRANKENSTEIN'S DOG

GOOSEBUMPS HorrorLand™

Also Available from Scholastic Audio Books

Goosebumps®

MOST WANTED

FRANKENSTEIN'S DOG

R.L. STINE

SCHOLASTIC INC.

No part of this publication may be reproduced, stored in a retrieval system, or transmitted in any form or by any means, electronic, mechanical, photocopying, recording, or otherwise, without written permission of the publisher. For information regarding permission, write to Scholastic Inc., Attention: Permissions Department, 557 Broadway, New York, NY 10012.

ISBN 978-0-545-41801-0

Goosebumps book series created by Parachute Press, Inc.
Copyright © 2013 by Scholastic Inc.

All rights reserved. Published by Scholastic Inc., *Publishers since 1920.* SCHOLASTIC, GOOSEBUMPS, GOOSEBUMPS HORRORLAND, and associated logos are trademarks and/or registered trademarks of Scholastic Inc.

12   11   10   9   8   7   6   5   13   14   15   16   17   18/0

Printed in the U.S.A.   40
First printing, August 2013

WELCOME. YOU ARE MOST WANTED.

Come in. I'm R.L. Stine. Welcome to the *Goosebumps* office.

Have a seat over there. Just move the pile of skulls onto the floor. I keep meaning to return them to their owners. But all skulls look alike to me. Know what I mean?

"OUCH!" Did Irving, my pet cobra, just bite you on the arm? Well, don't worry. That means he *likes* you.

No worries. Really. The venom won't paralyze you for half an hour. So we have plenty of time to talk.

Let me ask you a question while you can still move your lips. Who do you think is the *Most Wanted* monster of all time?

No. I wasn't thinking of your brother. Although, he's pretty high on the list.

And I wasn't thinking of the drooling, grunting monster creeping up behind your chair right now. Don't turn around. He's very shy. He hates being watched when he's preparing to pounce on a helpless victim.

The Most Wanted monster? I was thinking of Dr. Frankenstein's monster.

That monster was sewn together from pieces of bodies. Then a real human brain was stuffed inside his head. Victor Frankenstein built the monster — and let it escape. It terrified the villagers, who had to fight to destroy it.

That was a long time ago. Our story today is about Victor Frankenstein's great-grandson. Guess what? He's also named Victor Frankenstein.

Is Victor a mad scientist like his great-grandfather? Is he also building a monster?

A girl named Kat Parker will tell you the story. She's going to visit Victor Frankenstein because he's her uncle. You and Kat will find some surprises at her uncle's creepy, old mansion — surprises and terrifying danger.

And watch out for Frankenstein's dog. Sure, he looks cute. But is he man's best friend — or *monster's* best friend?

"Ouch."

The bus bumped over a rut in the narrow road. I gripped the seat in front of me and gazed out the dusty window.

We were riding through rolling green hills. Down below, I could see my uncle's village with its tiny stone houses and shops and slanting red roofs. From up here, it looked like a toy village, little doll houses, a village for storybook elves.

I suddenly felt all fluttery, and I had to force myself to breathe normally. Hey, this was totally exciting. A long flight over the ocean. Then an eight-hour bus ride to a distant village hidden in the hills to see my uncle, Victor Frankenstein. I couldn't believe it was happening.

My name is Kat Parker. I'm twelve, but I haven't traveled like a lot of kids.

My parents are teachers, and there are five of us in our family. So we don't have a lot of money.

When we go on family vacations, it's usually to a cabin at the lake a few hours from our house.

This spring, I had an idea for a project I wanted to do about my uncle Victor. So I wrote to him and asked if I could come visit for a week.

Uncle Victor and I are very close. I mean, I don't see him that often, and I've never been to his house. But he flies to the United States and comes to our house for holidays. And he and I spend hours talking about his science projects and all his wild ideas.

I know. He's a brilliant scientist and I'm just a sixth-grade girl. But I really think we have a lot in common. He's kind of my idol. I mean, I'd love to be a scientist and inventor like him when I'm older.

He spends all his time just dreaming up amazing things and then building them. How much fun is that?

And now the bus was following the road down, curving through the grassy hills to the village. And I was getting more excited with each bump in the road, each turn taking me closer to him.

I couldn't wait to tell Uncle Victor my project idea. I didn't tell him in my letter. I wanted it to be a surprise.

My plan was to record a video blog of his work. I wanted to show his laboratory and his office, where he works, where he thinks up his wonderful science inventions.

Yes, it's a school project. But it's also something I've dreamed of doing for a long time.

I pressed my forehead on the glass and peered out the window as we rumbled past a tiny one-pump gas station, then a feed store with bags of seed stacked in front, then a café with a blue neon coffee cup filling the front window.

The bus squealed to a stop at a corner. No bus station. Just a wooden bench with a man in overalls sharing his lunch with a brown-and-white mutt.

I gazed around but didn't see my uncle. I climbed into the aisle and pulled my suitcase down from the overhead rack. Then I made my way to the door, my heart pounding.

I was the only passenger getting off in the village. I thanked the bus driver. He gave a bored sigh and murmured, "Have a good one."

I stepped off the bus, and he closed the door and pulled away. I glanced around. The man and the dog on the bench both stared at me. Like I was a Martian or something.

Guess the village doesn't get many visitors.

A boy in baggy jeans and a long black T-shirt came out of a small grocery store carrying an ice cream cone. Two orange-and-white cats scampered across the road and disappeared into a narrow alley.

I shielded my eyes from the sun with one

hand. It was a hot summer day. The air felt dusty and damp.

No sign of Uncle Victor.

My suitcase was getting heavy. I set it down on the curb. My uncle promised he'd be here to greet me. But I wasn't surprised that he wasn't here.

Victor is forgetful sometimes. I mean, he's a genius scientist, right? He gets caught up in his work, and he just forgets about time.

I turned and peered up the street. No cars moving. I could hear voices from the café down the block. A young blond-haired guy leaned against the gas pump at the filling station, looking lonely and bored.

It's such a tiny village, I thought. *It can't be very far to walk to Uncle Victor's house.*

A sweet smell floated on the air. I saw a woman walk out of a bakery shop across the street. I hoisted up the suitcase and crossed to the shop to get directions to Uncle Victor's house.

A bell rang over the glass door as I pulled it open and stepped inside. I took a deep sniff. The air smelled like cinnamon. A glass counter displayed cakes and breakfast rolls. Coffee brewed on the counter beside it.

A white-haired woman with a round, red-cheeked face stood behind the counters. She wore a long white apron over a plain gray dress. She was chewing on a small brown chunk of bread. She watched me with narrowed gray eyes as I stepped close.

"Can I help you, miss?" Her voice was younger than her appearance.

"I . . . just got off the bus. Can you tell me how to walk to my uncle's house?"

She squinted harder. "Well, who's your uncle?"

"Oh. I'm sorry," I said. I could feel myself blushing. "Victor Frankenstein."

She dropped the bread onto the plate. Her mouth formed an "O" of surprise. "Don't go there," she murmured.

I wasn't sure I heard her correctly. "Excuse me?"

"Don't go up there."

I *did* hear correctly. "He . . . he's my uncle —" I started.

She raised both hands, as if pushing me back. "He's crazy. Like his great-grandfather before him," she said. "Up in that old mansion."

"If you could just tell me —"

"Building monsters. That's what he's doing," she said. She was breathing hard now, her face even redder than before.

I took a step back. I felt frightened. I didn't know what to say. "He — he's a scientist," I said. "He isn't —"

"Building monsters," she repeated. "No one is safe with him in town. No one. He's up in that mansion. Crazy as the first Victor Frankenstein all those years ago. Building monsters."

7

"You're wrong," I said. "That can't be true."

"Don't go there. I'm warning you." She waved me toward the door.

I spun away, pushed open the door, and stumbled to the street. She followed me outside.

"Oh!" I uttered a gasp as I saw that a crowd had gathered. A crowd of villagers, young and old. They formed a wide circle around me. They didn't look friendly.

"Wh-what's wrong?" I cried. My voice came out tiny and high.

"Who are you?" a woman shouted.

"She's Frankenstein's niece!" the woman from the bake shop announced.

"Go home!" a man shouted. I recognized him. The one with the dog on the bench. "Go home!"

The crowd took up the chant. "Go home! Go home! Go home!"

"We don't want you here!"

"Your uncle is a *monster*-maker! Your family isn't welcome in this village!"

"Go home! Go home! Go home!"

And then two angry young men — dark-haired twins — grabbed me by the arms.

"Hey, let go!" I cried. "What are you *doing*! Let go! Let go of me!"

2

"Let go! You're hurting me!" I cried. My legs felt weak and rubbery, but I struggled to pull myself free.

"Go home! Go home!" the crowd chanted. The faces were red and angry.

I tried to cry out for help. But my voice caught in my throat.

Suddenly, the twins let go of my arms. I stumbled forward, into a blond-haired boy. We both almost fell over. But he grabbed me by the shoulders and steadied me.

I pulled back. My heart raced in my chest. What was he going to do?

"You're okay," he shouted over the angry crowd. "Your uncle sent me. My name is Robby."

He spun angrily to the crowd and raised both hands for silence. It took a while for the chanting to end.

"Why are you doing this?" he shouted. "Why

are you trying to scare her? She's a visitor. Is that the way you treat visitors?"

I was still panting, gasping for breath. I stared at the crowd, silent now. But would they attack me again?

"If she's a Frankenstein, we don't like her," one of the dark-haired twins said. He had his fists clenched, his jaw tight.

"We don't like what her uncle is doing up there," his brother snarled. He pointed up the hill at the end of town.

"You are superstitious fools!" Robby cried. "He is a scientist. He isn't building monsters!"

Monsters?

Why did the villagers believe Uncle Victor was building monsters?

"Leave her alone," Robby shouted. "Show her some kindness."

He stuck his chest out, as if ready to fight them. But he didn't look tough. He was an inch or two shorter than me and kind of skinny. With his blond hair, pale blue eyes, and freckled nose, he didn't look like much of a fighter.

But the villagers backed away. The twin brothers glared at me. Then they turned and walked into the bakery shop. People muttered and shook their heads as they went off in different directions.

"Sorry about that," Robby said. "Are you okay?"

"I . . . guess," I replied. "Just a little freaked out. I didn't expect to be attacked by an angry mob." I wiped some dust off the front of my T-shirt.

"They're more frightened than angry," Robby said. He picked up my suitcase from the curb. "That's because they like to spread dumb rumors. They talk about your uncle as if he's some kind of crazed horror-movie scientist. But it's not true."

He motioned with his head toward the hill at the edge of town, and I started to follow him. "I think I know Uncle Victor really well," I said. "He's so quiet and shy."

Robby nodded. Our shoes crunched on the sandy road. We passed a small bank, another café, and a post office with faded travel posters in the window.

People stared at us from the café window. I felt a chill seeing their hard, unfriendly faces.

"My mom says Uncle Victor is kind of forgetful. And he gets wrapped up in his work," I said. "But he's too sweet to be a mad scientist."

Robby nodded. "Yeah. He seems like an okay guy." He shifted my suitcase to his other hand.

The sun grew hotter as we left town behind and started to climb the sloping hill. Tall grass tilted in every direction on both sides of the road.

As the road curved, a house came into view up high in the distance. It was huge and gray, and I

11

could see several chimneys towering over the wide, dark roof.

"Is that my uncle's house?" I asked, shielding my eyes from the sun.

Robby nodded. "Yeah. That's the Frankenstein mansion. It's very old. The house has been in the Frankenstein family for generations. I mean, it's ancient."

"Uncle Victor told me about it," I said. "But he never said it was as big as a castle."

Robby swatted a bee off his hair. The bee circled his face, then darted away. "Why'd you come?" he asked. "Just for a visit?"

"Well, yeah," I said. "I've never been here." The hill grew steeper. I had to hurry to keep up with Robby.

"And I have a project I want to do," I said.

He squinted at me. "Project? Like a science project?"

"No. I want to do a video blog. You know. About my uncle and his work. Show his experiments and have him talk about them."

Robby nodded. "For school?"

"Yes," I said. "And I'm hoping if it turns out really good, maybe it'll help me get a scholarship to this special science school I want to go to."

"Cool," he muttered.

I had another idea. "Maybe I'll do a video tour around the old house, too. Like something extra. I want the blog to be really good."

Robby said something in reply, but I couldn't hear him. A crowd of fat crows huddling in the tall grass began cawing their heads off.

Robby laughed. "They sound like the villagers."

The crows flapped their wings noisily but didn't fly away. Some of them watched Robby and me as we walked past.

As we neared the top of the hill, I could see the house clearly. It was built of smooth gray stone with black shutters on the sides of tall windows stretching up to a slanting roof.

Were those crows circling the chimneys high above us — or bats?

We stepped up to a tall metal fence. Robby set down the suitcase. Then he unlatched the gate. I led the way.

We had gone two or three steps when I heard the low growls. I stopped short and Robby bumped into me.

The growls became louder. I let out a cry as two snarling black dogs came furiously galloping across the vast front yard toward us.

They were big and tall, angry, red-eyed, their mouths open, teeth bared. Their backs were arched, ready to attack.

"Don't move," Robby said. "Guard dogs." He pulled a whistle that hung around his neck. "No problem. This controls them."

"Hurry!" I said. "Blow it!"

13

He raised the whistle to his mouth.

"Nooo!" I shouted as it slipped out of his hand. The whistle sank into the grass.

And the snarling dogs leaped at us, gnashing their pointed teeth.

I ducked and made a frantic grab for the whistle. My hand fumbled in the tall grass.

A shadow swept over me, and I felt a burst of wind on my back. One of the dogs leaped *right over me*. I heard it land with a hard thud behind me on the grass.

I found the whistle and wrapped my fingers around it.

Robby was wrestling with the other dog. The creature had Robby pinned to the ground, and it was standing on Robby's chest, snapping its teeth at his shirtsleeve.

The dog spun around and was preparing to leap at me again.

I raised the whistle to my mouth. And blew it with all my strength.

Silence.

The whistle didn't make a sound.

But the dogs went limp. Robby's attacker lowered its head and backed off him. The other dog uttered a long sigh. It shook itself, then turned and slumped toward the house.

I pulled Robby to his feet. His sleeve was torn, but the dog hadn't bitten his arm. He shook his head, as if shaking the attack from his mind.

"Close one," he murmured.

The tall front doors to the house swung open. Uncle Victor came running out. "Kat, are you okay?" he called.

"I'm fine," I said.

He wrapped me in a hug. "I'm so sorry. I meant to chain those dogs. But I got tied up in the lab and . . ." He pushed me back to take a look at me. Then he smiled and hugged me again. "Well, you sure got an exciting welcome. The rest of your stay probably won't be as exciting."

I laughed. "I hope not."

"It was my fault," Robby said. "I dropped the whistle."

"No. You were a hero," I told him. I turned to Uncle Victor. "Robby saved me from a crowd in the village."

Uncle Victor frowned and rubbed his chin. "Those people . . . They're very confused. And I guess they're bored. They spend their time making up horror stories about me."

"I'd better get home," Robby said. "See you, Kat." He turned and strode toward the gate.

"Thanks for your help," Uncle Victor called after him. Then he picked up my suitcase, and I followed him into the house. The two big dogs watched meekly as we passed, heads lowered.

The front hall was all black-and-white marble with an enormous sparkly chandelier high overhead. A stained glass window sent beams of light dancing over the walls.

"Wow," I murmured. "Uncle Victor, you never told me —"

A fluffy white dog came scampering into the room. A little guy, a terrier of some kind, with round black eyes half-hidden behind wisps of white fur, and an adorable pink nose.

The dog ran right past my uncle and padded up to me. It sniffed my jeans, then raised itself onto my legs, jumping for me to pick it up.

Uncle Victor laughed. "Poochie likes you," he said. "He's usually shy."

I bent and lifted Poochie into my arms. The dog licked my nose. I laughed. I'm ticklish. "Hi, Poochie." I raised my head to my uncle. "Seriously. He's so cute."

"He's totally spoiled," Uncle Victor said. "He really thinks he's boss here. And he *is*."

I gave Poochie a hug. His little heart was beating fast. His fur was way soft. I set him down and he trotted over to my uncle.

I took a moment to study Uncle Victor. I hadn't seen him since Christmas. He is tall and very thin. His wavy brown hair is mixed with gray. His square black glasses make his dark eyes look

17

very big. His face always seems serious to me, even when he smiles. I guess it's the lines on his forehead and the dark circles under his eyes.

I think he's in his forties. He dresses like an old man. He usually wears dress shirts and suit pants that are baggy and too big for him. Today, he had a white lab coat over his clothes.

"Why are you staring at me?" he asked. The light flashed over his glasses. I couldn't see his eyes.

"Because I haven't seen you for so long," I said. "I'm so happy to finally see your house."

He swept a hand back through his hair. "I'll take you to your room in a minute. First, I want you to meet Frank."

Our shoes clicked on the marble floor. He led me into the front room. The living room. The size of our gym at school.

"Frank? Who is Frank?" I asked.

Uncle Victor turned around. A strange, tight smile stretched over his face. "Frank is my *monster*," he said in a whisper. He leaned closer and whispered in my ear. "He's my monster, Kat. I've created a *monster*. And together, we're going to *rule the world*!"

I took a step back. Uncle Victor's hot breath was still in my ear.

His eyes were wild. And he still had that frightening smile frozen on his face.

The villagers are right about him, I thought.

But then he burst out laughing. "Kat? Did you really believe me?"

"I — I — I —" I stammered.

He squeezed my shoulder. "I'm not a mad scientist. Really. That was my horror movie impression. All those scary movies they made about my great-grandfather and the creature he built. I think they're a riot."

I could feel my face turning red. I should have remembered that Uncle Victor has a wild sense of humor. Why was I so ready to believe that he was a madman who created a monster?

He kept his hand on my shoulder and led me to the lab at the back of a long, carpeted hall. "I'm interested in artificial intelligence," he said.

"Computer brains. Robots that can think for themselves. Monsters aren't my thing."

He pushed open the door and we stepped into the lab. I nearly tripped because Poochie ran right over my feet. "Is he allowed in the lab?" I asked.

Uncle Victor nodded. "He's allowed everywhere. I told you — he's the boss."

A sharp alcohol smell invaded my nose. I coughed. The lab smelled like a doctor's office. The air was hot and damp.

The room was huge, with gray stone walls rising up two stories. A row of tiny square windows along the top let in the only sunlight.

I saw long tables with all kinds of computer equipment. A million cables and boxes and monitors. A table against the far wall held glass beakers with colorful liquids, a tangle of long glass tubes, and jars of chemicals. Some of the beakers were bubbling over low fires.

And at the end of the table stood a young, dark-haired guy. He had his back against the wall. His eyes were down, and he didn't look up when Uncle Victor and I entered.

"Hello," I called to him. But he didn't move.

Uncle Victor chuckled. "That's Frank," he said. "Don't expect him to greet you, Kat. I haven't powered him up yet."

I gasped. "He's . . . a robot? But he looks so real."

We walked closer, and I saw the glassy stare in the robot's brown eyes and the frozen expression on its face.

"I developed a new synthetic skin," Uncle Victor said. "It looks real, doesn't it? But I created it in the lab and molded it over his aluminum frame."

I stepped up close and rubbed my fingers over Frank's cheek. "Oh! It's warm."

Uncle Victor nodded. "The skin is self-heating. I'm very proud of that." He squeezed Frank's shoulder. "Actually, I give myself a pat on the back every time I work with Frank. I'm very proud of my creation. And when you see him in action, I think you will understand why I am so pleased."

I studied the robot. "I like his Grateful Dead T-shirt," I said. "It's really retro."

"I found it in a dresser drawer," Uncle Victor said. "It fits him pretty well, don't you think?"

"Better than those ratty cargo jeans," I said.

"Okay, okay. Forget his outfit. The best thing about Frank is his brain." Uncle Victor tapped Frank's head. "I've spent years and years building a brain for him that can think and even make decisions."

I blinked. "You mean —?"

"Frank doesn't need me to tell him what to do. He can make plans and choices on his own."

"Wow," I said. "That's amazing. Are you —"

I stopped because of a sudden loud noise. I heard a bump, then a thumping. I turned. It was coming from the back wall. It sounded like someone was knocking against the narrow gray door there.

Uncle Victor's cheeks turned red. "Don't pay any attention to that," he said. "It's nothing. Sorry it scared you, dear."

Another thump. Another.

"Is someone knocking on the other side of the door?" I asked.

"Just ignore it," he replied. "And when you're in the lab, always stay away from that door. Okay? Promise?" He hesitated. "It . . . it's where I keep my failures."

Did he mean there were robots on the other side of the door? Robots that didn't work right? Robots he kept locked up?

I didn't get a chance to ask. He walked over to the long table and picked up a beaker filled nearly to the top with a purple liquid. He poured some of it into a drinking glass and walked back to me.

"Kat, I've been so rude," he said. "After your long trip, you must be thirsty. Here. I made this especially for you."

He handed the glass to me. I stared at the purple liquid inside. "What is it?"

He smiled. "It's like that grape juice you used to like when you were little. I think you'll like it. It's very sweet."

I held it in front of me. The purple liquid gleamed in the light from the ceiling. Why was Uncle Victor watching me so intently? So eagerly?

I love my uncle. I knew he wouldn't give me anything that was bad for me. But why did he have that weird look on his face?

Finally, I raised the glass to my mouth and took a sip.

"Mmmm. It's good," I said.

I took a longer drink. It *did* taste like very sweet grape juice. I wiped my upper lip with my free hand.

Uncle Victor's smile grew wider. His eyes flashed behind his eyeglasses.

"Kat! It worked!" he cried. "It really worked. You're *invisible*!"

5

"Huh?" I nearly dropped the glass.

He took it from my hand. He laughed. "You believed me, didn't you!"

"Well . . . I . . . I . . ."

"You're too easy to fool," he said. "You fall for every one of my jokes. Just like when you were little." He finished the juice in the glass.

"My friends play tricks on me, too," I confessed. "I always believe everything. Mom says I'm *gullible*. I had to look that word up. I guess she's right."

"Well, maybe I can toughen you up," he said. "After a week with me . . ."

"I'll try not to believe a word you say!"

That made him laugh. He raised his right hand. "No more tricks. I promise."

I rolled my eyes. "Ha-ha. Seriously. I don't believe you."

His smile faded. He pushed his glasses up on his nose. "Do you want to see Frank come to life?"

"For sure," I said. I gazed at Frank's frozen face, his glassy eyes. His straight brown hair appeared to be real hair. "How do you power him up?"

"Simple. Flip a switch." Uncle Victor pulled up the left T-shirt sleeve. He lifted Frank's arm. "See?"

I leaned forward and saw the small metal switch in the robot's armpit.

Uncle Victor flipped the switch. Then he lowered the arm and pulled the T-shirt sleeve back into place. "Watch, Kat. He boots up quickly."

Frank blinked his eyes. His lips moved silently up and down. Not like a puppet's lips. They looked soft, and they moved like human lips. He twitched his nose. The shoulders rose, then fell, as if he was testing them.

"Good afternoon," Frank said. His voice was nice, a young man's voice, not a computer voice.

"Frank, what time is it?" Uncle Victor asked.

"Two-thirteen," Frank answered instantly.

Uncle Victor poured some of the purple juice into the glass and held it up to the robot. "Frank, are you thirsty? Would you like a drink?"

"No, thank you," Frank answered. "I'm a robot. I don't have a stomach, so there is nowhere for the juice to go."

"Do you have a tongue?" I asked him.

"My speech is a brain function," Frank replied. "I do not need a tongue to speak clearly. But I can use my tongue for *this*." He stuck out a pink tongue and made a rude spitting noise.

I burst out laughing. "Uncle Victor, does he have *your* sense of humor?"

My uncle seemed very pleased. "I tried hard to make him entertaining. I want him to be more human than any other scientist's creation. His brain is so highly developed, even I don't know everything it can do."

Frank turned his brown eyes on me. "I don't believe we have met," he said.

I blinked, surprised. "My name is Kat," I said. "I'm Victor's niece."

Frank nodded. "My name is also Kat," he said. "What an interesting coincidence."

Uncle Victor moved forward quickly and grabbed Frank's arm. "Your name is *not* Kat!" he shouted. "Correct yourself."

The robot stared hard at me. The lips moved silently.

"Correct yourself," Uncle Victor insisted. I could see he was upset.

"My name is Frank. Pleased to meet you, Kat."

Uncle Victor blew out a breath of air. "That's better." He turned to me. "He's not perfect. There are still some bugs."

"Kat, aren't you going to shake hands with me?" the robot asked. He sounded hurt.

"Go ahead." Uncle Victor motioned me forward. "He doesn't really have feelings. But he's programmed to *think* he has feelings. Shake hands with him."

I reached out my right hand. He raised his hand at the same time. He took my hand and squeezed it gently. We shook hands.

I pulled back to end the handshake, but Frank held on. He squeezed harder.

"That's enough, Frank," Uncle Victor said.

But the robot's hand clamped down tighter around mine. I could feel the hard metal under the skin. It started to hurt.

"Hey!" I cried out, struggling to free myself.

"Let go, Frank," my uncle growled.

The hand clamped tighter around my hand. Tighter.

I heard a *craaack*. A stab of sharp pain shot up my arm.

"Uncle Victor — do something! *Do* something!" I cried. "He's *breaking* my hand!"

I heard another *craaack*. The pain shot up and down my whole right side.

Uncle Victor dove forward. He hoisted up Frank's left arm and clicked the switch in his armpit.

The robot's hand loosened and slid off mine. Frank blinked two or three times. His head nodded forward, and his body slumped. He didn't move.

"Kat, I'm so sorry. I'm so sorry," Uncle Victor said. He took my hand gently. The skin was red, but the pain was fading. He moved the hand carefully in his hands, one finger at a time.

"Nothing broken," he said softly. "Must have been your knuckles cracking. I'm so sorry. Really. What a terrible introduction."

"It's okay," I said. "I just didn't expect —"

Uncle Victor pushed the glasses up on his nose again. He studied Frank. "I have some problems with him," he said. "I still have a lot to work on."

"Was he deliberately trying to hurt me?" I asked. I shook my hand in the air. It still stung a little.

"I'm not sure," Uncle Victor replied. "Sometimes he gets confused. It's like a blip in his brain. Like a bad circuit. And then sometimes . . ." His voice trailed off. He moved the robot's arm up and down. "Sometimes Frank acts angry."

"Angry? Seriously?"

He nodded. "Yes. Angry. I don't understand it. I didn't program him that way. I programmed him to have no emotions or feelings at all. So I don't understand how he could possibly be angry."

"Weird," I murmured. I didn't know what else to say.

The robot gazed blankly down at the floor.

"So be careful around him," Uncle Victor warned. "Most of the time, he's perfectly okay. But it's good to stay alert. And one other thing, Kat . . ."

"Yes?"

"Always make sure the lab door is closed. Always double-check to see that it is closed. Frank is my finest creation. I couldn't be prouder of this robot. But he definitely isn't ready to leave the lab."

Uncle Victor directed me to my room. I followed the winding staircase up to the second floor. I

29

found myself in a long, dark hallway. Tiny lights shaped like candles lined both sides of the hall but didn't cast much light. My shoes caught on the thick, faded carpet.

The walls were covered with big paintings of hunting scenes. I passed a painting of a dozen men on horseback chasing a herd of buffalo. The next painting had a man in a buckskin outfit with a knife raised in his hand, facing down an angry bear.

Did Uncle Victor choose these paintings? I wondered. *Or did he find them here when he took over the house?* They were all dark and frightening and violent.

The floorboards groaned and squeaked beneath the carpet as I walked, carrying my suitcase. Shadows stretched across the hallway floor as if reaching for me.

I was a little freaked. I mean, it looked like haunted-house-time up here. At least there weren't any cobwebs or skeletons lurking around corners.

I found my room at the end of the hall. A ceiling lamp cast bright light over a pretty, striped bedspread, a nightstand, two comfy-looking armchairs, a yellow dresser, and a small desk.

Uncle Victor had left a vase of purple tulips on the dresser. The tall window was open, letting in a warm breeze. The yellow curtains fluttered in the wind.

I set down my suitcase and hurried to the window to check out the view. Leaning out the window, I looked down on the side of the yard. A wilted flower garden and tall weeds everywhere, and a hedge that hadn't been trimmed in centuries.

I guess Uncle Victor didn't have any time for yard work.

I was up so high. Beyond the hedge, I could see the sloping green hills that led down to the village.

I turned away from the window, opened my suitcase on the bed, and started to unpack. I'd just started to pull out some shorts and jeans when I remembered my phone.

I pulled it out of my bag and started it up. I had strict instructions to call home and tell Mom and Dad I'd arrived safely.

I started to push my home phone number — then stopped. No service. No bars. I checked for a Wi-Fi network.

"Oh, wow. I don't believe it," I murmured to myself. Uncle Victor didn't seem to have any Wi-Fi.

I'll use his phone to call, I decided. I set the phone down on the little nightstand beside the bed. I could still use the phone to record my video blog.

I returned to my suitcase and started unpacking more stuff. I'd packed way too much. I

31

wouldn't need half the skirts and tops I brought. I could see we wouldn't be going out much.

I saw Poochie watching me from the door. "Don't stare, Poochie," I said. "It isn't polite."

And then I gasped when the little dog whispered: *"Be careful, Kat."*

"Huh?" I gazed down at the fluffy white dog. "Did you just say —"

Then I saw Uncle Victor standing in the doorway, half in shadow.

I burst out laughing. "I must be losing it. I just thought Poochie warned me to be careful."

Uncle Victor chuckled and stepped into the room. He had a purple stain on the front of his lab coat. "Poochie is a smart dog, but I haven't taught him how to talk yet."

His eyes went to the window. "I came to warn you about the bedroom window."

I turned. "The window? What about it?"

He crossed the room and pulled back the yellow window curtains. "See? The window is so low. It comes down almost to the floor. It might be easy to fall out."

I made a face at him. "I'm not five, you know. I haven't fallen out of any windows lately."

He frowned at me. "There are no window guards. If you fall, it's a steep drop to the ground." He pulled the window shut.

"But, Uncle Victor — I really like fresh air. I —"

He lowered his eyes to the dog. "I worry about Poochie, Kat. He isn't as smart as you think he is. He might venture to the window, see a squirrel outside, and jump out."

Poochie rolled onto his back and stretched his legs in the air.

"You're right. I'm sorry," I said. "I'll be careful about the window."

I had a sudden idea. I picked up my phone and pressed the video icon. I raised the phone to my eye and aimed it at Uncle Victor. "Go ahead. Pull back the curtains again," I said. "This might make a nice start for my video."

His eyes went wide behind his glasses. "Excuse me? Video?" He raised the sleeve of his lab coat and hid his face. "What are you doing?"

I lowered the phone. "Uncle Victor, I didn't know you were so shy."

"I'm not shy," he said. "If I'm going to be on camera, I need my makeup and hair stylists. I need to know my lines. Where is the script?"

"Funny," I said. "I guess I should have told you about it. See, I thought I'd do a video blog. To help me get a science scholarship."

He bent down and rubbed Poochie's belly. "A

video blog of me straightening the window curtains?"

I rolled my eyes. "No. Seriously. I want to record you at work. You know. Show what you do in the lab. Have you demonstrate Frank and maybe some of your other robots. It'll be, like, *A Scientist at Work.*"

He made a pouty face. "And I thought you came to spend time with your dear old uncle."

I set down the phone. "Of course I did. But the video blog could help me *so much.* You'll do it, right?"

"Of course, dear," he said, giving Poochie one last rub. He stood up. "Oh. I almost forgot. I invited Robby to come back. You liked him, right? It's probably not a good idea to visit the village. So I asked him to come here and keep you from getting lonely."

"Thank you," I said.

I studied him as he wiped the dog fur off the front of his lab coat. *Uncle Victor is so sweet,* I thought. *Why do the villagers hate him so much?*

Sadly, I would soon find out.

I spent the morning playing with Poochie in the backyard. Poochie loved the freedom of being outside. But it made me nervous. The weeds and shrubs were so high, I kept losing him. He would disappear for five or ten minutes. And he never came when I called him.

Finally, I picked him up in both hands and carried him back into the house. Robby was sitting at the long wooden table in the kitchen. Uncle Victor was slicing a freshly baked chicken for sandwiches.

Robby wore a long black T-shirt over baggy khaki shorts. He kept tapping the tabletop with both hands, pounding out a rhythm. He looked up as I carried Poochie in. "Hey, Kat. How's it going?"

"Good," I said, setting the dog down. "Poochie and I were playing hide-and-seek in the back. I didn't really want to play that game. But Poochie *loved* hiding from me in the weeds."

"He has a devilish side," Uncle Victor said. "He's not as sweet as he looks." He set the sandwiches down on the table. "Lunch is served. If you don't mind, I'm going to take mine to the lab."

"See you later," I said. I took a seat across the table from Robby and we dug into the sandwiches.

"This house is awesome," Robby said. "Whenever I'm in here, I feel like I'm in a movie."

I snickered. "A horror movie?"

"Well . . . kind of." He swallowed. "What do you want to do today?"

"It's a beautiful day," I said. "I'd love to take a walk down to the village."

Robby shook his head. "No way. You know your uncle wants us to stay away from the village." He took another bite of his sandwich.

"Then let's explore the house," I said. "There are so many rooms and so many long, twisting halls. Maybe we can get lost. You know. Spend days marooned in a distant hallway. Wandering from room to room, calling for help. I could video the whole thing. It could be awesome."

Robby squinted at me. "You're weird."

I laughed. "I was just messing with you," I said. "I always try to make things more interesting than they are. Mom calls me a drama queen." I snickered. "She doesn't mean it as a compliment."

Robby grinned. "Maybe we should bring these sandwiches with us in case we get lost for days."

I scooted my chair back. "Come on. Let's go. I really am excited to see this house. When I was little, Uncle Victor liked to tell me ghost stories that happened here. He said ghosts walked the halls at night, clanking their chains."

Robby shook his head. "Why do ghosts always have to clank chains?" he said. "If they are ghosts, couldn't they just slip out of their chains?"

"Maybe we can find some ghosts, and we'll ask them," I replied.

Robby and I headed down the back hall that led away from the kitchen. I liked him. He was easy to talk to, and he had a nice laugh. I think he liked me, too. But I couldn't really tell.

The back hall led to Uncle Victor's lab. But before we reached the lab, we turned and climbed a wide, carpeted stairway. The air grew warmer as we climbed. A tall window, covered in dust, let in pale sunlight.

I gazed down a long, straight hall with rooms on both sides. The only windows were at the ends of the hall. So the sunlight gave way to deep shadow as Robby and I walked.

My eyes stopped on a tall, black stone statue. A man, standing straight and stiff, a long cape down his back. One hand was raised. It carried a human skull in its palm. The statue's eyes stared toward the stairway, as if guarding the hall.

"I think that's Victor's great-grandfather," Robby said. "The original Victor Frankenstein."

"Cool dude," I said. "A little scary. I mean, he looks kind of angry. Like he doesn't want to be standing here."

"He caused a lot of trouble in the village," Robby said, gazing at the skull.

"Maybe the statue comes to life at night," I said. "Frankenstein walks the halls, looking for his monster."

Robby clapped his hand over my mouth. "Stop making up stories, Kat. You're giving me the creeps."

I pulled his hand away. "Let's check out these rooms."

We started exploring, room by room. The first room appeared to be a guest bedroom. But the thick cobwebs over the window and the layer of dust on the bedcover showed that it hadn't been used in a long time.

The next room had shelves from the floor to the ceiling filled with old radios. I mean real antiques. The kind you see in old movies. There were dozens of them. A back shelf held cartons filled with radio parts, glass tubes, and wires.

"I guess Uncle Victor likes old radios," I said.

Robby sneezed. "Wow. So much dust in here," he said.

"Race you to the next room." I bumped him out of the way and darted out the door. I beat him easily into the next room and glanced around.

This room was huge, with tall, dirt-smeared windows on one wall. Bookshelves covered the other three walls, and the shelves were filled with old books, their dark covers worn and tattered.

Two ratty-looking armchairs and a small table stood in the middle of the room. Cone-shaped lights hung from the ceiling over the two armchairs.

"A library," Robby said. He walked over to one shelf. His eyes ran down the spines of the old books. "All science books. Wow."

I spotted an old trunk at the far wall. I walked over to it, bent, and pried the lid open. I was greeted by the sharp aroma of mothballs. And a gross sour smell. Like bad meat.

Robby stepped up beside me. He reached into the trunk and lifted out a wrinkled white shirt. "Check out the ruffled cuffs."

I pulled out a silky red vest and a rhinestone mask. "It's costumes," I said. "Weird old Halloween costumes."

"Your uncle has some strange collections," Robby said.

"I know. A long time ago, he told me he likes to collect *everything*. He said that's why he loves this old mansion. There's room for all his junk."

Robby sneezed again. He pinched his nose with two fingers. "This old stuff totally stinks. Close the trunk."

I squatted down, stuffed the mask and vest back inside, and slammed the trunk shut. I started to climb to my feet. But Robby bumped me back to the floor.

"Race you to the next room!" he cried, and took off.

"Not fair!" I yelled. I scrambled after him.

I was surprised to find the hall covered in darkness. Clouds had swept over the sun, and the two tall windows at the end of the hall were solid gray. It took a few seconds for my eyes to adjust to the dim light. Then I stepped into the next room.

"Robby?"

I glanced quickly around. No sign of him. Squinting into the gray light, I saw a pool table in the center of the room and a row of tall stools.

"Hey! Robby?"

No answer.

I turned and trotted back into the hall. "Robby?" My voice came out muffled in the long, dark hallway. Behind me, I could see the caped statue of Victor Frankenstein, black against the gray light, still watching the stairs.

Did he go into the next room?

My shoes snagged on the ragged carpet as I walked to the next open doorway. The light was cold and silvery, light enough to cast long shadows in front of me.

"Robby? Are you in here?"

I peered into the room. At first, I didn't see him. I saw only the tall stacks of magazines and newspapers piled nearly to the ceiling.

But then I lowered my eyes — and my breath caught in my throat.

I saw him. Robby. Sprawled facedown on the floor, arms spread.

Not moving. Not moving.

I opened my mouth in a frightened scream.

But my scream was cut off as someone grabbed me from behind.

"Let GO of me!"

The words burst from my throat.

I lurched forward and tore free of the hands holding me. I spun around. "Robby?"

He nodded. "Don't be scared, Kat."

"But — but —" I sputtered.

He motioned to the figure sprawled facedown on the floor. "Did you think that was *me*?"

"Why — yes," I stammered. "I saw you. There on the floor, and —" I realized I was still shaking.

Robby strode into the room and bent down over the fallen figure. "It's just a robot," he said. He lifted one arm, then let it fall limply back to the floor. "It's a broken robot."

"It . . . looked so lifelike," I said, starting to feel a little more normal. "I really thought —"

Robby shook his head. "Your uncle isn't a very good housekeeper. Why did he leave a broken robot lying here?"

"Good question," I said.

Robby motioned down the hall. "Let's see what surprises there are in the next room."

I sighed. "No, thanks. I mean, really. I think maybe I'm through exploring for now."

We turned back to the stairs. The statue of Victor Frankenstein kept its guard. I rubbed my hand over the cape as we passed by. The stone felt surprisingly warm.

I shivered. I kept seeing those arms and legs sprawled on the floor. This old house was definitely creepy. But that was one reason I came. I wanted to explore my uncle's world. I wanted to capture it all on video.

"Too bad you didn't bring your phone up here," Robby said, as if reading my thoughts. "You could have started your video blog."

"I know. I left it in my room," I said. "Maybe tomorrow."

We made our way down the stairs, half-walking, half-sliding down the creaking wooden banister. At the bottom, we found ourselves facing the door to Uncle Victor's lab.

"Let's go in and see what he's doing," I said. I knocked on the door. No reply. I knocked again, a little harder.

I brought my ear close to the door and listened. I couldn't hear any activity in there.

"Uncle Victor? Are you in there?" I called.

Silence.

I turned to Robby. "He must have gone out. Have you ever seen the lab?"

"No," Robby said. "Never."

I turned the knob and pulled open the door. "Come on," I said. "It's amazing. I'll show it to you."

Robby held back. "Are you sure we should go in there?"

"Of course," I said. "What could happen?"

10

I led the way into the lab. The lights were all on. Computer screens flickered. Big glass tubes of chemicals bubbled and fizzed.

No sign of Uncle Victor.

The air smelled like my dentist's office. A sharp, clean medicine smell.

"It's like we stepped into an old horror movie," Robby said. "A mad scientist uses this lab to turn animals into humans." He picked up a test tube containing a purple liquid. "One drink of this, and you become a werewolf!"

"Put it down," I said. "My uncle is *not* a mad scientist."

He tilted the test tube to his mouth and pretended to drink the purple liquid. Then he opened his mouth wide and let out a wolf roar.

"You're not funny," I said. "See all these computers? Uncle Victor isn't making werewolves. He's learning about artificial intelligence. He's making robots that can think for themselves. Robots that are *definitely* smarter than you."

"Sorry," Robby said. He set down the test tube. "Just joking, you know."

"Well, you sounded like the villagers. All that mad scientist talk isn't funny."

Robby walked around the long table filled with beakers and tubes and huge glass containers of colorful liquids. "Wow," he murmured. "Wow. This lab is awesome."

I followed him over to the table of computers. He counted them. "Twelve? Your uncle has twelve computers going at once? What's *that* about?"

"About being a genius," I said.

I don't know why, but I felt like defending Uncle Victor to Robby. I didn't like the mad scientist jokes. I knew how serious and smart my uncle was.

Robby just kept muttering "wow." He was impressed.

He walked back to the lab table and gazed at the brightly colored chemicals running through tubes, fizzing in their glass containers. "I wonder what he's mixing up here," he said.

"I don't know," I said. "Wish he was here. He could tell us. He could —"

I stopped when I heard a soft thud. It was followed by a low groan. Like an animal in pain.

"What was *that*?" I cried.

Robby motioned to the narrow door at the back wall. "It came from back there, I think."

We heard another groan. Then a rustling sound. It was definitely coming from the other side of that door.

Robby started toward it.

"Stop," I called. "Uncle Victor said to stay away from there."

"Huh?" Robby spun back to me. "Stay away?"

"Yes," I replied. "He said he keeps his failures in there."

Robby scrunched up his face. "His failures? What does that *mean*?"

Another thud against the door. Then silence. Silence, except for the bubbling of the chemicals in their tubes and beakers.

I spotted Frank, my uncle's most advanced robot, standing by the window. The robot stood stiffly, arms hanging limply at his sides, eyes shut.

"Robby, check this dude out," I said, motioning to Frank. "It's Uncle Victor's most awesome robot. He named the robot Frank."

Robby stepped up to the robot. He raised its right hand and shook hands with it. "How do you do, Frank. Nice to meet you. Are you smarter than me like Kat says?"

Robby let go of the hand and it dropped back to Frank's side.

"He's so smart?" Robby said. "He can't even answer me."

"He's shut off, dummy," I said.

Robby laughed. *"Who's* the dummy?"

"When he's powered up, he's totally human," I said. "Seriously. He talks like a human, and he moves around naturally. He answers your questions. He can really *think.*"

Robby stared at Frank's human-looking face. Then he turned to me. "Go ahead, Kat. Power him up. I want to see him come alive."

"I . . . I don't think we should," I replied.

Robby frowned at me. "You mean you don't know how to power him up?"

"I know how," I said. "I just don't think Uncle Victor would like it. Frank can be a little dangerous. I mean, he squeezed my hand and —"

"Just for a minute," Robby said. "Half a minute. Come on. I want to see him open his eyes and say something. That's all. Then you can turn him right off."

"Hmmmm." I thought hard about it. "Okay," I said finally. "Just for a few seconds."

I stepped up to the robot. I lifted his arm and pushed back the sleeve of his Grateful Dead T-shirt. My fingers found the switch in his armpit — and I clicked him on.

11

I took a step back. My heart was pounding. I knew I shouldn't be doing this.

Why did I listen to Robby? I guess I wanted him to like me.

Nothing happened for a few seconds. Then the robot blinked his eyes. His mouth twitched. He turned his head and stared hard at me, as if booting up his memory. Trying to remember me.

"Wow. He moves," Robby said.

"Of course I move," Frank replied in his soft whisper of a voice.

Robby and I burst out laughing. I'm not sure why. I guess we both were nervous.

Frank stretched his arms over his head. He tilted his head from side to side, as if stretching his neck. It was just like a human waking up.

Robby stood next to me. He didn't talk. He just stared at the robot as he came to life.

Frank finally took his eyes off me. "How are you, Robby?" he asked.

"Hey," I said to Robby. "You told me you've never been in my uncle's lab. How does Frank know your name?"

Robby's cheeks turned pink. "Uh . . . he probably heard your uncle phone me to come over here and keep you company."

I turned back to Frank. "Is that true?" I asked. "How do you know Robby's name?"

The robot's shoulders moved up and down, as if it was shrugging. "I have many names in my memory bank. My face recognition system works with my memory cells."

I didn't really understand that answer. My heart was still beating hard. I wanted to switch the robot off. Before Uncle Victor came back. He seemed nice now, and calm. But I remembered how Frank got violent for no reason at all.

"Frank, can you show us around the lab?" Robby asked.

Frank nodded. "Yes. I can give you both a short tour. What would you like to see?"

"No," I said, stepping between Robby and Frank. "I think we have to stop right now, Robby."

"Just a few more minutes," Robby said. "I want to see —"

"I can heat up some chemicals and give you a really big surprise," Frank said. His eyes blinked rapidly.

51

"No way!" I cried. "I mean, not now, Frank. Robby and I have to go. Uncle Victor will be home soon. I think —"

Robby laughed. "Kat, why are you so stressed? Frank wants to show us what he can do with chemicals."

I scowled at Robby. "You said we'd turn him on for just a few seconds. I don't think this is right."

"Okay, okay," Robby muttered, raising both hands like he was surrendering.

"You can show us your trick with chemicals later, Frank," I said. I reached for Frank's arm to click off the power switch.

But he ducked to the side.

I gasped in surprise. He moved so quickly.

I made another grab for his arm. But he slid out of my grasp. And then he took off, running to the open lab door.

"Hey, stop!" I screamed.

The robot's shoes pounded the hard lab floor. He ran with amazing speed.

Robby and I ran after him. "Stop!" I screamed again. "Frank, stop! STOP!"

12

The robot darted through the open doorway and slammed the door behind him.

Were we locked in? No. I grabbed the handle and pushed the door open.

Frank was halfway down the long hallway, running hard.

"Get him!" I cried to Robby. We both squeezed through the doorway at the same time and began to run side by side down the hall.

"Frank — come back! *Frank!*" My shout came out hoarse and frightened.

The robot paid no attention. He dove around a corner and disappeared from view.

I tripped over a hole in the carpet and stumbled into the wall. Robby stopped to grab my arm and pull me back to my feet.

"He ... he's getting away," I stammered. "Uncle Victor will be furious."

"He won't get far," Robby said.

We both started to run again, past room

after room. I saw a mouse staring, perched on a bed in an empty guest room. Window blinds rattled in front of an open window in the next empty room.

Robby and I turned the corner. I squinted into the dim light down the hallway.

"Oh, nooo," I moaned. "Where is he? Where?" No sign of Frank.

Robby pointed to the row of doors along the right side of the hall. "He must be hiding in one of those rooms."

"But *why*?" I cried. "Just to get me in trouble?"

"Maybe he wants his freedom," Robby said. He gave me a gentle push. "Come on. Start searching."

We ran to the first room. The door was closed. I pulled it open and peered inside. I saw cardboard cartons piled to the ceiling. Several boxes marked FRAGILE. No Frank.

Robby was already on his way to the next room. I saw him stop. His eyes gazed down the hall. He pointed. "Kat — look!"

At the end of the hall, I saw the front door to the house. Frank stood at the front door, struggling with the lock.

"He ... he's trying to get *out*!" I gasped. "Stop him."

Robby and I took off, running as hard as we could. Frank turned and saw us coming. He fiddled frantically with the door.

I heard him snap the lock. He grabbed the handle and pulled the door open.

"Noooo!" I cried. "Frank — stop! Frank — don't go outside!"

I ran past Robby. I was *so close* to Frank. I took a deep breath. Stretched out my hands to grab him. And dove to tackle him.

I let out a scream as I tripped. No. Something tripped me.

My head swung around as I went down. I saw Poochie at my feet. I'd tripped over Poochie.

I landed hard on my elbows and knees.

And stared helplessly as the robot hurried out the front door.

13

Robby reached the door first and darted outside. I pulled myself to my feet, stepped around Poochie, and followed him.

Frank was running across the front lawn, heading toward the gate. Robby ran after him.

"Where are you *going*?" I screamed at Frank. "Please — stop! Don't go to the village. I'm warning you, Frank. Don't go to the village!"

He'll terrify the villagers if he shows up there, I thought.

What will the frightened villagers DO to him?

Frank was nearly to the front gate. Robby and I were running hard, leaning forward, arms outstretched. But I could see we weren't going to catch him.

Then I heard a heavy thud of footsteps behind us.

Startled, I swung my head around — and saw the two guard dogs galloping after us.

Their heads were lowered, mouths open in angry snarls, teeth bared. Ready to pounce.

Up ahead of us, Frank stopped. He turned to the dogs. I could see his eyes go wide.

"Look! Frank is afraid of the dogs," I said to Robby.

The robot stood frozen as the dogs came charging across the lawn.

I stepped up to Frank. Raised his arm. Found the switch in his armpit — and clicked him off.

His body went stiff. His eyelids shut.

The dogs barked excitedly as they prepared to attack.

"Robby —" I cried. "The whistle! Blow the whistle! Hurry!"

Robby reached around his neck, then uttered a gasp. "I don't have it, Kat. *You* took it — remember?"

Oh, no. Oh, nooooo.

"I . . . I don't have it!" I stammered. "It's up in my room."

"We are so . . . doomed," Robby murmured. "Doomed."

14

Robby and I both cried out in terror as the dogs leaped to attack us.

I heard a sound from the house. A high squeal of a dog bark.

To my shock, the dogs appeared to stop in midair. They landed hard on the ground. Panting, they gazed at one another.

I turned to the house and saw Poochie on the front stairs. He had his head tilted back and was barking furiously.

The huge guard dogs lowered their heads. Their arched bodies, still ready to attack, slumped and appeared to collapse. One dog shuddered, shaking its whole frame.

Poochie continued his shrill bark.

The dogs turned and trudged away, their ears down, heads lowered.

"I don't believe it!" I cried. "They're afraid of little Poochie."

"I'll bet your uncle trained them to back off when Poochie barks," Robby said.

"Maybe," I said. "Uncle Victor *did* say Poochie was the boss."

I stared at Poochie. He had finally stopped barking. He had his head raised, as if in triumph.

I realized I was shivering. I could still feel the blood pulsing at my temples. I let out a long breath. "Close one."

Robby mopped sweat off his forehead with the back of one hand. He swallowed hard. "I'm going to have nightmares about this."

The guard dogs had retreated to the side of the front walk. But they kept their eyes trained on us.

I looked back at Poochie. But the little dog had disappeared into the house.

I motioned to Robby. "Come on. We have to get Frank back to the lab."

Robby frowned at the robot. "What a jerk. Why was he running away?"

"Don't think about it," I said. "Hurry. I'll take the head. You take the feet. We'll carry him —"

Robby grinned. "Why don't we just click him back on and let him *walk* back to the lab?"

"Ha-ha. Funny," I said. "No *way* I'm ever turning him back on without Uncle Victor around. I think we learned one thing. Frank can't be trusted."

I wrapped my hands around Frank's head. His skin felt like human skin. Robby took the feet, and we hoisted the robot off the ground. He was heavier than I thought he'd be. We carried him like a log to the house.

The guard dogs watched us in silence. Their ears drooped. They still looked frightened.

Poochie is one tough little dude, I thought.

Into the house. I carefully closed the front door behind me. Then we slowly made our way down the long hallway.

"This guy weighs a ton," Robby said. "Must be all the circuits and controls inside."

"I think his brain weighs *two* tons," I said. "His head is like a *bowling ball.*"

"Careful. Don't drop him," Robby warned.

I shifted my hands on the robot's head and stepped up to the lab door. "If Uncle Victor ever finds out what we did . . ." I didn't finish my sentence.

I struggled with the door. "I . . . think it's locked," I said. "I think we're locked out." A wave of dread rolled down my body. *Uncle Victor will never trust me again.*

Gripping the robot tightly, Robby and I traded places. I watched Robby push the door with his shoulder. He pushed with all his strength.

Then I burst out laughing.

He spun around. "What's so funny?"

"Try pulling," I said.

He grabbed the handle and pulled. The door opened easily. He shook his head. "Okay, okay. We're both a little tense."

We hoisted Frank up and carried him into the lab. We set him down near the window where we found him. He stood stiffly with his eyes shut. I tugged down his shirt and brushed his hair back with my hand.

"There. He looks okay," I said. "Let's get out of here before Uncle Victor finds us."

I started to the door — but stopped as Poochie scampered into the lab. He darted across the room and stopped to sniff a dark spot on the floor near the computer table.

"Poochie, let's go," I called. "Out. Out of here. We have to go."

The little dog ignored me. He sniffed the spot, then moved quickly under the table with all the bubbling chemicals.

"No. Get out of there," I said. I hurried toward him, ready to pick him up. "You'll get in trouble, Poochie. You shouldn't be in here."

I reached for the dog, but he slipped out of my grasp. He let out a short *yip* and scurried back to the computer table.

I turned to Robby. "Don't just stand there. Help me catch him."

Robby laughed. "The little guy is a speed demon." He grabbed for Poochie and the dog scampered away. "I think he's playing a game with us now, Kat."

"I don't like this game," I said, moving toward Poochie. "He's going to get us in trouble."

I moved to trap the fluffy white troublemaker in the corner. But he saw me coming and ran behind Frank. "Come out of there," I said. "Stop it, Poochie. First Frank, now you. You're making me angry."

The dog let out another *yip* and darted toward the chemical table. "Enough!" I cried.

I dove for him. Missed. And bumped the table hard. The whole table shook.

"Unnh," I groaned as pain shot up my side.

I turned to see one of the glass beakers topple over. A thick green liquid came pouring out . . .

. . . pouring out . . .

. . . pouring onto Poochie.

Poochie uttered a growl as the green chemical splashed onto his back, spreading over his white fur.

I gasped. "Oh, no! What have I *done*?"

And as I gaped in horror, the dog began to grow.

15

The dog made weird growling, grunting noises. He rolled his head around and twitched his back.

I grabbed the glass beaker and stood it back up. Too late. The green chemical had formed a wide puddle on Poochie's back. And it dripped thickly down his sides.

Robby stepped up beside me, and we both watched as the dog twitched and grunted — and grew.

"This . . . isn't happening," Robby murmured.

But it was. Standing on all fours, Poochie had been less than a foot tall. But now, the fluffy white fur appeared to puff up. As if someone was blowing it with a hair dryer.

The dog twisted uncomfortably. His little black eyes gazed up at me.

I jumped back. "Robby — he's stretching. He's —"

"He's nearly as high as my *knees*!" Robby cried.

The head ballooned. The ears stretched as if they were rubber. The tail grew longer, and the whole body plumped up . . . wider . . . wider . . .

"Oh, no. Oh, no. Oh, no." I pressed my hands to the sides of my face. "I don't believe it!"

I took another step back. The dog almost reached my waist, and he was still growing. The fur puffed up and the legs stretched . . . stretched. . . .

"He's as big as a sheepdog!" Robby cried in a trembling voice. He grabbed my shoulder. "Kat — what are we going to do?"

The big dog shook himself. Green liquid splashed off his back.

"M-maybe if we wash the stuff off . . ." I stammered.

Poochie let out a loud growl. He shook himself again, sending more splashes of green chemical flying across the lab.

"Let's try it," Robby said. "Let's wash the chemical off. Maybe he'll stop growing."

"But, how —" I started.

Robby grabbed the dog's big head with both hands. The head was as big as a soccer ball! "Help me, Kat." He started to tug Poochie toward the sink in the corner.

I bent down and grabbed the dog's back legs. I started to shove him forward. But my hands slipped — and slid over the thick fur on his back.

"Oh!" I raised my hands quickly. Too late. I touched the green gunk.

Robby still gripped Poochie's head. He raised his eyes to me. "Are you okay?"

"No!" I screamed. "No. I'm *not* okay! The green gunk! I touched it! I touched it!"

"Oh, wow." Robby's face filled with horror.

I staggered back. "I . . . I'm growing!" I screamed. "Oh, help! Help me! What am I going to do? I'm GROWING!"

16

Holding on to Poochie's head, Robby squinted at me. "No, you're not," he said.

I gasped. "Huh? What do you mean?"

"You're not growing, Kat. Look at yourself. You . . . you just panicked, that's all."

I was panting like a dog. I tried to slow my breathing. I gazed at my hands, sticky with the green chemical. I lowered my eyes to my shoes. "You're right," I murmured. "I'm okay. I'm not growing. Sorry."

"Hurry," Robby said. "To the sink."

I bent down and grabbed Poochie from behind. The dog tried to pull free. The poor guy must have been totally confused.

I grabbed his back legs and pushed hard, sliding him across the room. Robby tugged at the head, pulling hard with both hands.

As I pushed, I saw that Poochie had grown even taller. He was now higher than my waist.

Uncle Victor loves this dog, I thought. *He's going to be furious when he sees what I've done.*

"It isn't going to work," I said. "Pouring water on him . . ."

"We have to try," Robby insisted.

Somehow we dragged the big dog to the sink. "Okay. Let's lift him up and put him in the sink," I said.

Robby squinted at me. "Are you serious? He must weigh two hundred pounds."

I spotted a bucket against the wall. And I saw a drain in the floor. "Okay. Hold him still. Hold him over the drain."

I filled the bucket with water. Poochie watched me, bobbing his big head hard, struggling to free himself from Robby.

I tilted the bucket over him and let the water pour down his back.

The dog stopped struggling. The water loosened the thick green chemical. Some of it ran into the drain on the floor.

"Is it working?" I cried in a high shrill voice.

"I can't tell," Robby said. "Keep going."

I poured another bucket of water on Poochie. Then another.

Poochie shook his head hard. He sent water and chemical droplets flying in the air.

I stared down at him. "Robby, I think it's working. Look. Does he look smaller to you?"

Robby studied the dog. "Maybe. Come on. More water. Let's wash off all the gunk."

I poured another bucket of water over Poochie. Then I found a brush and scrubbed his fur with it. The chemical was dissolving, melting away. It was all slipping down the drain.

And Poochie . . . Poochie was definitely shrinking. He was no taller than my knees now.

He had grown shorter — and calmer. He stood very still with his head lowered and let me pour another bucket of water over his back.

"Look at him," I said. "He knows we're helping him."

"It's working! It's really working!" Robby cried. He pumped his fists in the air. "He'll be back to his normal size by the time your uncle returns."

Suddenly, I had an idea.

"Hold him still," I said. "I'm going to run and get my phone. I want to record this for my video blog. I want to show Poochie shrinking. It will be awesome. No one will believe it."

"Better hurry," Robby said. "He's almost normal size already."

I jumped to my feet. My clothes were soaking wet from all the splashing water. But I didn't care. Poochie growing huge, then shrinking, was *amazing*. And I wanted to get at least a little of it on video.

Wiping my hands on the legs of my jeans, I ran out of the lab. I hurried down the long hall, turned into the next hall, and found the stairway that led to my room.

I took the stairs two at a time, my hand bouncing over the wooden banister. My heart was pounding by the time I reached the second floor.

Into my room. I glanced at the dresser. Where did I leave my phone?

I spotted it on the bed table beside my unmade bed. I crossed the room, grabbed it, turned it around — and uttered a shocked cry.

"Oh, no. Noooo."

The glass was cracked. A crisscross of cracks across the front of the phone. "Oh, wow. I don't believe it," I murmured.

I raised the phone closer to my face — and realized it was destroyed. Totally crushed.

17

Gripping the phone in my hand, I hurried back to the lab. "Robby — look!" I cried. I pushed it into his face.

He was squatting down, rubbing Poochie dry with a red-and-white checked towel. "Poochie is back to his sweet little self," he said. "See?"

"Good," I said. "But look. Look at this." I waved the phone in front of him. Robby dropped the towel. As soon as he was free, Poochie scampered out of the lab.

Robby took the phone from my hand and examined it. "It's busted," he said. "Totally smashed. How did that happen?"

"I — I don't know," I stammered. I balled my hands into tight fists. My anger burned my throat. "Who would do this? Someone had to be in my room."

Robby turned the phone over in his hand. "But that's crazy. There's no one else here, Kat. Your uncle's housekeeper is away."

"Someone was in my room," I insisted. I was so upset, my voice was shaking. "Someone wrecked my phone." I let out a long whoosh of air. "Robby, do you think someone was sending me a message? Am I in danger here?"

Uncle Victor returned to the house in time to prepare vegetable soup and lamb stew over rice for dinner. After we sat down at the kitchen table, Poochie stood by my uncle's chair, waiting for handouts. Poochie was quite a beggar.

"I hope you and Robby had fun with Poochie today," Uncle Victor said, spreading the napkin over his lap. He wore baggy khakis and a plaid flannel shirt. It was strange seeing him out of his white lab coat.

"Uh . . . yeah," I said. "We played with Poochie a little."

No way I was going to tell my uncle that I spilled a green chemical on the dog and turned him into a giant.

We spooned up our soup for a while. It was hot and very tasty. But I didn't have much appetite. I had only one thing on my mind. I planned not to bring it up until after dinner. But I just couldn't hold it in till then.

"Uncle Victor, take a look at this," I said. I slid my phone across the table.

He set down his soup spoon and wiped his mouth with the napkin. "What's wrong, dear?"

I motioned to the phone, and he picked it up. He studied it for a long moment. Then he raised his eyes to me. "Goodness. What happened?"

"It's smashed," I said through gritted teeth. I suddenly felt like crying. But I forced it back. "Totally smashed."

He held the phone close to his face, turning it over and over in his hand. "I . . . I don't understand, Kat. Was there some kind of accident?"

"Accident?" I cried. "Look at it. Uncle Victor, someone was in my room. Someone broke my phone."

His cheeks turned red. He shook his head. I could see he was thinking hard. "But there's no one else in the house," he said finally. "Myra, my housekeeper, is away till next month visiting her sister. You and I are all alone here, dear."

"But — but —" I sputtered.

He patted my hand. "Kat, it must have fallen off your bed table and cracked."

My breath caught in my throat. I stared at him. *How did he know it was on my bed table?*

Uncle Victor slid the phone across the tablecloth to me. "So sorry," he murmured. He patted the back of my hand again.

Then he bent and lifted Poochie off the floor. He cradled the dog in his arms and stroked the thick white fur on his back.

I suddenly pictured giant, sheepdog-sized Poochie. The dog stared at me as if reading my thoughts. I felt guilty for not telling Uncle Victor what had happened this afternoon. But I just didn't want to get in trouble my first day in the house.

Uncle Victor shook his head. "So sorry," he said again. "Now you can't do your video blog, dear. I know how disappointed you must be. I'm very disappointed, too."

I nodded. But then I had an idea. "Maybe I can buy a new phone in the village," I said. "There must be a shop there that sells phones."

Uncle Victor set Poochie down on the floor. He brushed white fur off the front of his shirt. "I don't think you should go to the village, Kat," he said softly. He locked his eyes on mine. "It's not a friendly place."

"But, Uncle Victor —" I started.

He pushed back his chair and jumped to his feet. "I'm sorry. I have to get back to the lab. I'll be working late tonight."

He took a few steps toward the hall, then turned back. "I have just one request for you, dear," he said.

I squinted at him. "Request?"

He nodded. "Yes. Don't ever leave your room at night."

18

I blinked. His request shocked me. "Why?" I said. "What's *that* about? Why can't I leave my room?"

"I bring the guard dogs in at night," he replied. "If you are out in the hall, they might think you are an intruder."

"Excuse me? You bring them into the house?"

He nodded. "My work is very important. And I worry about intruders. The villagers. They are very superstitious people. I worry they might come here and try to destroy my work."

"Uncle Victor," I said, "do you ever talk to people in the village? Do you ever try to explain to them that you're building robots with computer brains — not monsters?"

He sighed. "I can't talk to them, Kat. They won't listen. They are afraid of science, afraid of anything new. They only think of the first Victor Frankenstein. And they remember his monster."

He turned and strode down the hall toward his office in the back of the house. *He has changed*, I thought.

Whenever he visited our house, he was lively and fun. He made silly jokes, and we always laughed a lot. I guessed that his work had made him tense. He really didn't seem like the same person.

With a sigh, I gathered up my broken phone and made my way upstairs to my room. The old wooden stairs creaked as I climbed, and I heard soft footsteps behind me.

I turned to see Poochie following me. "Are you coming to keep me company?" I asked.

He let out a *yip*, turned, and scurried back down the stairs.

"You're weird," I said, shaking my head.

I stepped into my room. The air felt cold and damp. I decided I'd better sleep in a sweater tonight.

I turned and closed the heavy wooden door behind me. I tried to lock it, but the lock was broken. I stood at the door for a moment, listening to the silence out in the hall. I shuddered, thinking of those two vicious guard dogs patrolling the halls at night.

I forced myself to think about something else. I thought of Mom and Dad back home. I wanted to drop them an e-mail. Or maybe post something on their Facebook page.

But, of course, I couldn't. My laptop was useless since Uncle Victor had no wireless or phone connection up here.

Of course, he had a dozen computers in the lab. But he probably wouldn't want me using one.

So, I sat down at the desk facing the window. I found paper and envelopes in the top drawer. Sitting on the edge of the squeaky old leather desk chair, I wrote a long letter to Mom and Dad.

I told them I was fine and Uncle Victor was taking good care of me. I told them how hard he was working and about the robots he was building.

Of course, I didn't tell them about spilling a chemical on Poochie and making him grow huge. I did tell them about Frank the robot escaping. But I made it sound funny.

Then I told them about my broken phone. I asked them to rush me another phone as fast as they could. *Please send it overnight,* I wrote. *Without a phone, I can't record my video blog about Uncle Victor. And my whole trip will be ruined.*

I sealed up the letter, and I was addressing the envelope when I heard a sound at the bedroom door. A scraping sound. I dropped the letter and listened.

I heard a *thump*, then more scraping.

A chill rolled down my back. I pictured the two attack dogs. Pushing their way into the room.

I glanced around frantically and spotted the whistle on the dresser where I'd left it. I jumped to my feet, dove for the dresser, and grabbed up the whistle.

Another scratching sound. Soft pawing.

"Poochie? Is that you?" I cried in a tiny voice. "Poochie?"

Gripping the whistle in my hand, I crept to the door. I listened. Silence now.

"Poochie? Are you out there?"

I grabbed the knob and carefully pulled the door open a crack. Squinting into the dim light, I saw a man hunched at the wall, half hidden in shadow.

"Wh-who are you?" I stammered. I squeezed the doorknob, ready to slam the door shut. "Who are you?"

His face slid out from the shadow. His dark eyes glowed. "I'm Victor Frankenstein," he said in a whisper. "Who are *you*?"

19

I gasped.

He took another step toward me.

I could see him clearly now. He was lanky like my uncle. And his face was serious and dark-eyed as my uncle's face.

But he didn't wear the black, square-framed eyeglasses. I never saw Uncle Victor without them. And his dark hair was bushy and unbrushed. Not like my uncle's thinning brown hair.

He wore a white lab coat over dark pants. His shoes were heavy-looking with raised heels. Not at all like Uncle Victor's worn black shoes.

"You — you're not my uncle," I blurted out. My voice sounded hollow in the long hallway.

"Yes, I'm Victor Frankenstein," he rasped. He took another step toward me.

I let go of the doorknob and backed away, shaking, frightened.

His face was pale. Something was wrong with it. It was too long. Kind of twisted.

"You're not," I insisted. "You look like my uncle. But —"

He moved forward quickly and brought his face close to mine.

"Get out of here!" he cried in a hoarse whisper. *"Get away from here while you still can!"*

"Huh? Wh-what do you *mean*?" I choked out.

"Run. Get away — as fast as you can!"

A choked gasp escaped my throat. "Why are you *saying* that?" I cried.

His dark eyes flashed. His pale face appeared to ripple in the dim light. As if he was in a mirror. As if he wasn't really standing there in front of me.

He didn't answer my question. I heard rapid footsteps in the hall.

Uncle Victor appeared suddenly, his eyes wide with alarm. His white lab coat flapped behind him as he burst into my room.

He grabbed the other man by the shoulders and held him in place. "How did he get out?" he cried. "I was in the lab. I didn't see him escape."

"Who — who *is* he?" I stammered.

"I am Victor Frankenstein," the man said.

Uncle Victor uttered an angry growl. He lifted the man's arm and reached inside his shirtsleeve. He found the power switch in the armpit and clicked it off.

A robot!

His eyes shut. His body stood stiffly in place, arms lowered at his sides. Uncle Victor held on to the shoulders, as if expecting the robot to come to life again.

"One of my failures," he explained. He scrunched up his face. "I don't know how he got out. I'm really sorry if he scared you, Kat."

"Only a little," I said. "He — he said he was you. For a second, I was confused. I —"

"He looks a little like me," Uncle Victor said. He turned the robot's face from side to side with one hand. "But I think I'm better looking, don't you?"

We both laughed.

"But . . . why did he say he was you?" I asked.

"I gave him my name," Uncle Victor replied. "As a joke." He brushed back the robot's hair. "But he never worked properly. His brain isn't right. He says crazy things."

"Yes. He told me to run away," I said. "He said I should run away as fast as I could."

Uncle Victor chuckled. "Well, maybe you *should*. That's not bad advice, with *these* crazy escaped robots walking the halls."

He hoisted the robot off the floor and tossed it over his shoulder. "I'm going to carry him to the failure room. He won't bother you again."

He turned and started down the hall toward the stairs. The robot's arms dangled down his back, bouncing as Uncle Victor walked.

Halfway there, Uncle Victor turned to face me. "Be sure to keep your door closed — okay?"

"No problem," I said. "No problem at all."

I realized I was shivering. From the cold air slipping in through the old window? Or from my scare with the creepy robot?

I finished addressing the letter to my parents. Then I climbed into bed and pulled the heavy covers and bedspread up to my chin.

After a while, I felt warm and cozy. I was just about to fall asleep when I heard another sound on the other side of the bedroom door.

Scratching. Clawing.

Go away, I thought. *Please — go away!*

But the clawing continued. Animal claws scratching at the wooden door.

I lay there under the heavy covers wide awake, too frightened to move. Too frightened to see who was clawing at my door.

20

The next morning at breakfast, I lied and said I'd slept well.

I blamed myself for acting so scared. I knew it was probably Poochie scratching the bedroom door. The poor dog was being friendly. He probably wanted to cuddle up for the night. And I just lay there, shivering, not moving.

Well . . . I'm going to be brave from now on, I told myself.

I swallowed a forkful of scrambled eggs. Uncle Victor made them just the way I like them — dry, not too runny. We had discussed the right way to make scrambled eggs the last time he visited my family. It was so sweet of him to remember how I liked them.

But I was determined to be tough with him today.

"Uncle Victor, I really need to go to the village," I said.

He lowered his coffee mug and frowned at me. His eyes flashed behind his square eyeglasses.

"I don't want you going there alone," he said. "I don't have to remind you, dear, what happened when you arrived. Robby said you had a pretty scary welcome from our village neighbors."

"I'll run there and run right back here," I said. "No one will see me. I promise."

Uncle Victor shook his head. "Not a good plan, dear," he said. "I have to go out today. Maybe you and I can go to the village together tomorrow or the next day. Why do you want to go?"

"I have a letter to mail," I said.

"A letter?"

I nodded. "Yes. I wrote to my parents. I thought maybe they could send me a phone. I'm wasting so much time. I really want to make that video about you. You have overnight delivery here, right?"

"Yes," he said. "No problem. You don't have to risk going to the village, Kat. Just give the letter to me." He climbed to his feet. "I'm going out now. I'll mail it for you."

I hurried to my room and brought him the letter. He tugged on his long raincoat. The weather was windy with storm clouds low in the sky. "See you later." He waved to me and disappeared out the front door.

I finished my breakfast. I felt restless. I wasn't

scared to be in the house alone. I just didn't feel like staying indoors today.

Poochie watched me as I got dressed in jeans and a sweater. "I'm going to the village," I told him. "Just to explore. I'll be careful. And I'll be back before Uncle Victor even knows I went."

The dog tilted his head to one side, trying to understand me.

"I'm going to go in disguise," I said. I slid on my gray hoodie and pulled the hood up over my head. It wasn't much of a disguise. But it covered up some of my face.

The dog followed me to the front door. He stared up at me expectantly.

"I'm sorry, Poochie," I said. "I can't take you with me. I'm in a real hurry. Maybe some other time?"

He tilted his head again. It made me laugh. He was trying so hard to understand me.

I pulled open the front door. The strong wind almost blew the door shut. Ducking my head against another strong blast of air, I crept outside and shut the door behind me.

I was happy to see the two guard dogs chained to a tree at the side of the house. I stepped down the front stairs — and saw a big trash can on its side near the wall. The wind must have toppled it over. Trash was spilling out onto the grass.

I reached down and started to lift the can back up. "Whoa." I stopped with a startled cry. And picked up something I saw in the trash.

A letter. My letter to my parents. Ripped in half.

21

I jammed the torn letter into my jeans pocket. Then I tightened the hood around my head and made my way to the front gate.

With a clap of thunder, the sky opened up and heavy sheets of rain poured down. The big raindrops slapped the ground hard. The wind made the water splash around me like ocean waves.

Maybe I won't go to the village today, I decided.

I had a lot to think about as I hurried back into the house, shaking the rain off my hoodie.

I thought hard about Uncle Victor. He had always been my favorite uncle. He was so smart and quick and funny. And he really seemed to like me a lot. When he came to visit, he always spent more time with me than with my mom and dad.

He also loved the idea of my visit to his house. At least, he *said* he loved the idea in his letter. And he seemed totally happy to see me when I arrived. And eager to show off his robot and his lab.

So . . . Why was my letter ripped in half and thrown in the trash? Why was my phone smashed?

I told Uncle Victor I'd asked my parents to send a new phone in the letter.

Maybe he doesn't want me to have a phone. Maybe he doesn't want me to make a video blog of him and his work.

But that wasn't like Uncle Victor at all. Not like him in any way.

He always said what he meant. He never held back with me.

If he didn't want me to make a video, he would have told me. He would have said, "Kat, my work is too secret. I'm not ready for people to know about it. Please don't make any videos."

But the phone was smashed, and the letter was in the trash. And he acted as if everything was perfectly okay.

Not like him. Not like Uncle Victor at all.

I was still puzzling over the whole thing when Robby came to visit an hour later. I took his rain slicker and tossed it into the front closet.

He shivered. His blond hair was wet and matted to his forehead. "Wow. This storm is *rocking*," he said. "What's up with you?"

"There's something weird going on here," I said. "My uncle isn't acting at all like my uncle.

I think he has a big secret he doesn't want me to find out."

Robby snickered. "You sure you're not dreaming up stuff because you're bored here?"

I held up the two pieces of my torn letter. "I'm not imagining it," I said. "Look. He tore up my letter home."

Robby squinted at the letter. "Weird."

I stuffed the two pieces back in my jeans pocket. "My uncle said he'll be away all day. That will give us time to do some exploring."

He blinked. "Exploring?"

A chill ran down my back. This was supposed to be a fun visit with my uncle. But now I was truly frightened. Did I really want to find out what my uncle was hiding?

We walked into the kitchen. I found some hot chocolate mix in a cupboard and made steaming hot chocolate for us both. The hot drink soothed me. I started to feel a little calmer. Calm enough to think clearly.

"I just feel there's something very wrong here," I told Robby.

He wiped a smear of chocolate off his upper lip. "Like what?"

"Last night, a robot was walking the halls. It looked a lot like Uncle Victor, and it said it *was* Uncle Victor. Don't you think that's way creepy?"

Robby thought about it. "Well . . . he's a scientist. And he's experimenting with robots, right?"

"Uncle Victor isn't like himself. I hardly recognize him, Robby. He . . . he's acting strange."

He stared at me. I could see he didn't know what to say. He didn't know my uncle like I did. "You think —" he started.

But I interrupted. "I think maybe he's gone crazy or something," I said. "I know I could be making up a wild story. But, what if he's building *dozens* of robots? An *army* of robots. All named Victor Frankenstein."

Robby scrunched up his face, thinking hard. "And the villagers know about it? And that's why they're so angry and frightened of Victor?"

"Maybe," I said. "I just know that —"

I stopped talking. The words caught in my throat.

A *horrifying* thought flashed through my mind.

"Kat? Hey, Kat?" Robby reached across the table and squeezed my hand. "What's wrong?"

I swallowed. "I . . . uh . . ."

"You just went totally pale," he said.

"I suddenly had a thought," I said. "I mean, why was Uncle Victor so eager for me to come here? He's never invited me before. Does he have some kind of plan for *me*? Does he plan to *use* me somehow with his army of robots?"

"Whoa. That's *too* crazy," Robby said. "Stop, Kat. You're scaring yourself. You have to stop dreaming up crazy ideas. You have to —"

"But I'm frightened, Robby," I said, gripping the hot chocolate mug with both hands. "I'm really frightened."

He stared at me. "What do you want to do? Go home?"

"I can't go home," I said. "I want to find out what's going on here. I want to know what Victor is doing here with all these robots. I want to find out why he doesn't want me to make a video. And why he has changed so much."

Robby nodded. "So . . . what do we do?"

I jumped to my feet. "We go back in the lab," I said.

22

I started to the hall. But I turned back to see Robby still sitting at the table. "Hey, are you coming with me?" I asked.

He shook his head. "I . . . don't know."

I pressed my hands on my waist. "What's your problem?"

"I don't think we should go back in that lab."

"Because?"

"Because of what happened last time. You spilled that green gunk and turned Poochie into an elephant? Did you forget?"

"I didn't forget," I said. "We'll make sure Poochie isn't around this time. Where *is* the dog, anyway?" I glanced around. Poochie was sound asleep, sprawled on his side under the kitchen table.

"Come on, Robby," I said, motioning him to the kitchen door. "Don't be a wimp."

"I'm not a wimp," he snapped. "I just think it's dangerous in the lab. And —"

"What if *I'm* in danger?" I cried. "What if Uncle Victor really has gone crazy and has all kinds of insane plans?"

"Okay, okay." He climbed to his feet. Then he tilted the mug to his face and drank the last drop of his hot chocolate. "I'm coming with you. But I think this could be a major mistake."

We didn't speak as we made our way down the long back hall to the lab. Our footsteps echoed against the stone walls. As we came near the lab, the air smelled like alcohol. Like a doctor's office.

The lab door was closed. I grabbed the knob and turned it. I started to pull the door open, but Robby grabbed my wrist.

"Let go," I said.

"Just think about it for a minute," he said. "What are we going to find in there?"

I tugged my wrist free. "I don't know. I just know Uncle Victor is doing something very strange. And I need to find out what it is."

I gazed down the hall. No sign of Poochie. He must have still been asleep in the kitchen.

I turned back to Robby. "Are you coming in with me?"

And then I suddenly realized the truth. I suddenly realized why Robby was trying to keep me out of my uncle's lab.

I spun around, jabbing my finger on his chest. "I get it," I said. "You're a robot, too!"

He made a startled, choking sound and backed away from my stabbing finger. "Huh? Now *I'm* a robot? Seriously?"

I nodded. "I get it now. You're a robot. You don't want me to go into the lab and learn the truth."

"Whoa. Kat — listen —"

"My uncle put you here to spy on me," I said. "And to keep me here."

"No way!" he cried. "You've gone totally mental, Kat. You're wrong. You're way wrong." He took another step back.

"Okay," I said. "Prove it. Prove that I'm crazy. Raise your arm. Go ahead. Raise your arm, Robby. Let me see your armpit."

He wrapped his arms around his chest. "I don't have to," he said angrily. "I came over here to be a friend. That's all. That's the truth."

"Go ahead. Do it," I said. "Let me see your armpit. What are you afraid of?"

"I'm not afraid," he said. "I just —"

I grabbed his arm and shoved it high. Then I pulled up his T-shirt sleeve and stared at his armpit.

"Oh, wow," I murmured.

23

No power switch. Just an armpit.

I let go of his arm, shaking my head. "Sorry," I said. "I owe you an apology. I'm really sorry."

He tugged down his T-shirt sleeve. "Glad I passed the inspection," he muttered, rolling his eyes.

"Can you blame me?" I said. "I'm going to be seeing robots in my dreams if I don't find out what's going on in this house."

"Well, I'm not a robot," he said. "I'm a human."

I turned back to the lab. "Are you coming in with me or not?"

He frowned. "Yes. I'm coming with you. But I'm not happy about it."

I turned the knob and started to pull the door open again. Robby stepped up beside me. "Just don't knock over any chemicals this time," he said.

"Ha-ha." I poked him in the ribs.

"I'm not joking," he said.

I pulled the door open halfway. The lab was dark. The sharp alcohol aroma washed over me. I heard the hum of the computers and a soft, bubbling sound.

A chill of fear swept down my body.

Something bad was happening here. Why else would my uncle smash my phone and toss my letter in the trash? He had a secret he wanted to keep.

I fumbled on the wall until I found the light switch. I clicked it on, and lights lit up all around the lab.

I turned to Robby. "Quick — close the door before Poochie runs in."

He closed the door carefully and made sure it latched. He gazed tensely around the big room. "This place totally creeps me out," he said. "Especially being here without your uncle. If he comes home and finds us —"

"He said he'd be away all day," I said. My voice echoed in the big room. "Stop hanging by the door and let's explore this place."

Robby took a few steps toward me, then stopped. His eyes went wide. He pointed across the lab.

I turned and saw something moving quickly toward us. It took me a few seconds to realize it was Frank.

The robot's eyes were locked on me. His mouth was frozen in a tight scowl. He swung his arms stiffly as he trotted across the room.

"Why are you in here?" Frank demanded. His voice was a shrill squeal, like chalk on a blackboard. "Kat and Robby, why are you here?"

I started to lie. I started to say we were looking for Uncle Victor.

But then I thought: *Why should I lie to a robot?*

"We just want to look around," I said. "We won't touch anything. I promise."

"You must leave. You must leave now," Frank said, lowering his voice to a growl.

"But, Frank —" I started.

"Your uncle left my power on so I could guard the lab from intruders," Frank said. His eyes didn't stray from mine. "You are intruders. You must leave now."

He moved in front of Robby and me. He stretched out both arms, blocking our path.

"Intruders — leave now."

"Frank, please —" I said.

"Frank isn't my name!" the robot screamed. "Frank is my *nickname*. My name is Victor Frankenstein!"

I gasped.

The robot pushed out his hands and grabbed me by the shoulders. An angry sizzling sound escaped from his head. He squeezed my shoulders hard, holding me in place.

Then it tightened its grip . . . tightened. Until pain shot down both sides of my body.

"STOP!" I shrieked. "Let me go! Get OFF me!"

I struggled and twisted and squirmed. But I was no match for the robot's inhuman strength.

"Ouch! You're HURTING me!" I wailed. "Let GO! Let GO! What are you DOING? Let GO of me!"

24

I twisted hard. I tried to kick the robot.

But he lifted me off the floor. His hands tightened, and I squealed in pain.

"Frank — please. Why are you doing this to me?" I cried.

"I will hold you till your uncle returns," he replied. "Do not try to fight me, Kat. I have been given great strength."

I turned to Robby. He stood frozen by the lab door. His eyes were wide with fear. One hand gripped the doorknob, as if he was ready to escape.

"Robby — help me!" I cried. "He — he's *hurting* me! Do something!"

Robby hesitated for a second. He took a deep, trembling breath. Then he pushed himself away from the door.

He lowered his head as he came running. He opened his mouth in a loud cry of attack.

Robby stormed into the robot, giving him a hard head-butt in the side.

Startled, the robot let out a high-pitched squeal. He toppled over, carrying me down to the floor with him. Its hands loosened their grip, and I rolled away from him. .

Robby stood breathing hard, hands on his knees.

The robot jumped quickly to his feet and dove at Robby.

Robby cried out and dodged to the side. Frank sailed right over him.

Before Frank could regain his balance, Robby drove another hard head-butt into the robot's back.

Frank toppled to the floor, arms and legs spread. Robby jumped on top of him. He turned breathlessly to me. "Quick — Kat. His arm. Grab the power switch."

My shoulders still ached from the robot's tight grasp. I lurched forward. Dropped to my knees beside the robot.

Frank bucked and struggled to push himself up. But Robby didn't budge from his back.

I grabbed the robot's arm and twisted it up. I found the power switch in the armpit.

I grabbed it between my thumb and forefinger. And pushed it down.

I mean, I *tried* to push it down.

I held the arm still with my right hand. And tried the switch again with my left.

Tried to push it. To click the robot off. Pushed. Then pulled. Then pushed again.

"It . . . it's *stuck*," I moaned. "Robby . . . I can't turn him off."

25

Frank twisted hard and sent Robby flying off his back. My hand shot out from the robot's armpit.

Frank raised himself to his knees and swung his shoulder into Robby. Robby toppled into the side of the computer table. He let out a cry of pain.

The robot uttered an angry growl.

Robby ducked under the table. "Look out, Kat!" he cried.

The robot jumped to his feet and turned on me. "Violence is forbidden," he said in a flat, mechanical voice. "I am not programmed for violence. You have broken my laws. You have gone against the rules that I obey. I must control you now."

I gasped. "Control me? What do you mean?"

"I must control you both. You have gone against my programming. My brain is hurting from your violence."

He stepped toward me.

"You will pay now. You will pay, Kat."

His eyes had sunk into his head so that I saw solid white eyeballs. Steam sizzled from the sides of his head.

He moved forward, forcing me toward the wall.

I glanced all around. I searched for a way to escape. But he was pushing me back rapidly, forcing me to the table with all the beakers and bottles of chemicals.

"You must pay. You must pay." He kept repeating the words as if he was broken, stuck.

I bumped the table. Then I gasped as I heard pounding on the door on the far wall.

The sound appeared to startle Frank. He spun away from me for a second and gazed at the door.

It gave me a chance to escape. But how?

I was pressed against the lab table. If I tried to run, he could grab me easily.

I heard more thumps on the narrow gray door. A muffled cry from behind the door.

Frank turned to me.

I saw Robby, still under the lab table, holding his side. "Robby and I will leave," I said. "Let us go. We haven't done anything wrong. Let us out of here."

"I am the guardian," he said. "You are the intruders. I will control you now."

He moved forward, his arms outstretched.

Panic tightened my throat. I struggled to breathe. The robot had superhuman strength. What did he plan to do to me?

My gaze darted over the lab. My eyes swept over the bottles and tubes and beakers of colorful chemicals.

It took a few seconds to find what I was looking for. The beaker of green liquid. The liquid I spilled on Poochie that made him grow into a giant.

I kept my eyes on Frank as I reached behind me. I wrapped my fingers around the beaker and raised it off the table.

My plan? Simple. To pour the green chemical over my head. To grow huge and be big enough to stop the robot from attacking me.

Yes, it was a crazy idea. The green gunk didn't make me huge the day before. But I figured that was because I only had a tiny bit on my hands. If I poured the whole beaker over me . . .

Another hard bump on the door in back. This time, Frank ignored it. He strode closer to me. He was only inches away.

I raised the beaker high — and started pouring the liquid over my head.

It oozed over my hair and dripped onto my shoulders. It felt sticky and thick.

I emptied the whole beaker onto my head. Then I turned to face Frank.

"Back off, Frank," I said. "You'll lose this fight."

I stiffened my body. Tightened my hands into fists. And waited.

Come on, Kat. Grow. GROW. Hurry up and GROW.

26

I wasn't growing. I wasn't growing at all.

Frank grabbed me around the waist and started to lift me off the floor.

Robby jumped out from under the table and stormed up behind the robot, ready to try to fight him again.

I squirmed and twisted and tried to free myself. *Grow. Grow!*

Why wasn't I growing?

"I am the guardian," Frank said, as if in a mechanical trance. "Must control the intruders."

I couldn't battle his incredible strength. He raised me higher off the floor.

"What are you going to do?" I screamed. I had a dreadful thought that he was going to *heave* me across the room.

"Frank — put her down. Put her down *now*."

At first, I thought Robby had shouted those words. But I quickly realized the voice had come from the door.

Holding me in the air, the robot froze.

I turned and saw Uncle Victor step into the lab. He was in his overcoat and carried a large black briefcase in one hand. He dropped the briefcase to the floor and hurried across the room.

"Drop her, Frank," he ordered. "Set her down nice and easy."

The robot obeyed. As soon as my shoes hit the floor, I twisted free and ran beside Robby.

Uncle Victor marched up to Frank, who stood stiffly, staring straight ahead. "Intruders . . ." the robot said. "Intruders . . ."

My uncle reached under his arm. Grabbed the power switch tightly — and tugged it hard. Frank let out a wheezing sound as he powered down.

"Kat, I warned you about this robot," Uncle Victor said. "He's very smart. But he has problems. And —"

He stopped. Behind his glasses, his eyes bulged and he stared hard at me. "Your hair. What happened? Is that shampoo? Your hair is sopping wet."

"I — I —" How could I explain? Finally, I just blurted out the truth. "Yesterday, I poured that green gunk on Poochie, Uncle Victor. And he grew huge. So, today I poured it on me. I wanted to grow big so I could fight off the robot."

He studied the empty beaker. "You wanted to grow big?"

"Why didn't it work?" I said. "Why didn't it change me?"

Uncle Victor burst out laughing.

Robby and I just stood there, waiting for him to stop laughing.

Finally, he shook his head, still smiling, and said, "Wrong beaker, Kat. That's the hand soap I use when I finish work."

"The *what*?" I cried.

He started to laugh again. "You just poured a bottle of soap on your head." He pointed across the table. I saw a green beaker nearly hidden by a tangle of yellow tubes. "That's the Growth Chemical over there."

I touched my hair. Wet and sticky and matted together. I knew I looked ridiculous.

Uncle Victor's smile faded. "You and Robby were in my lab because . . . ?"

I decided to be honest. "Because we were looking for answers. There are some strange things going on here, and we wanted to find out —"

Uncle Victor nodded. "Yes, indeed. There certainly are some strange things going on here, dear. But you don't have to sneak around. I'll be happy to explain everything to you. You're my favorite niece, after all."

"I'm your *only* niece," I muttered.

He chuckled. "Well, no matter. You're my family. I trust you." He guided me to the door. Robby followed.

"Tell you what," Uncle Victor said. "Robby, you'd better get home. Your parents will be wondering where you are. And, Kat, you go upstairs and wash your hair. And when you come down, I'll tell you everything you want to know."

I squinted at him. "Everything?"

He nodded. "Everything. And I'll tell you about the plans I have for you. Very big plans. Very important."

A chill of fear ran down my back. "You — you have plans for me?" I stammered. "You had me come here for a reason?"

A sly smile crossed his face. "Maybe."

27

It took a long time to shower out the soap from my hair. The whole time, I kept thinking about my uncle and what he said about having plans for me. Should I be afraid? Should I be *terrified*?

No. My uncle didn't seem angry that Robby and I had entered the lab when he wasn't there. Mainly, he just laughed about me pouring hand soap on my head. He thought that was a riot.

He had his same crazy sense of humor. I *couldn't* be in danger.

Or *could* I?

I couldn't get Frank out of my mind. In a way, the robot really was a monster. He was cruel and strong, and couldn't be controlled. He really did want to hurt Robby and me for invading the lab.

I wondered if Uncle Victor made him that way. Maybe he wanted a cruel, hard robot to protect his lab.

At least he admitted that strange things were going on. I couldn't wait to hear him explain.

I fluffed my hair dry with a bath towel and tossed the towel onto the bathroom floor. I had a million questions to ask my uncle. Would he really answer them all?

Poochie greeted me at the bottom of the stairs. He rolled onto his back and wouldn't move until I petted his stomach for a long while. As I rubbed his stomach, he shut his eyes and mewed like a cat. Cute.

I found Uncle Victor in the kitchen. He was wearing his white lab coat. He had prepared a plate of cookies and a pitcher of iced tea. I sat down at the table, but he motioned me back on my feet.

"Follow me," he said. "We can have our talk in my secret room." He carried the cookies and iced tea on a tray and led the way down the back hall.

Again, I felt a tingle of fear. *Secret room?* "Are we going into the lab?" I asked.

No. He stopped short of the lab and unlocked a black door. I followed him into a long, narrow room. It looked like some kind of control room.

A row of big TV monitors filled one wall. On the long table beneath the monitors stretched a row of several desktop computers. They were all blinking and flashing with screens filled with numbers.

"My spy room," Uncle Victor said with a smile. He set down the food tray. Then he took a seat in front of the monitors and motioned for me to sit beside him.

"What do you spy on?" I asked. I took a cookie and sampled it. Chocolate chip. I was suddenly way hungry.

"Everything," he said.

He pushed some buttons, and the TV monitor in front of us flashed to life. As it came into focus, I could see his lab next door. I saw the table with all the chemicals. And I saw Frank standing at stiff attention in one corner, eyes half shut.

"You can watch the lab from in here?" I asked.

He nodded. "And I keep a recording of every minute in the lab. It's important. My work is so hard and so complicated. I need to keep a visual record of what I have done."

I took another cookie and stared at the screen.

Uncle Victor pushed some more keys on the computer in front of him. "Here, Kat. I think you'll find this interesting."

The screen blinked and went blank. When the picture returned, I could see the door of the lab open. Robby and I came walking in. Robby glanced excitedly all around. You could see how amazed he was by the awesome equipment.

"This was yesterday," I said. "You saw us in the lab. You saw everything, right?"

He nodded, eyes on the screen. He made the picture fast-forward.

I watched myself bump the table. Saw the beaker of green liquid topple over. Saw the chemical pour onto Poochie.

"You — you knew what happened," I stammered. "You knew the trouble Robby and I got into in the lab."

He patted my hand. "I have to know everything, dear," he said softly. "My work . . . It's too dangerous. I have to have my eyes on the lab at all times."

"But — but —" I sputtered.

He handed me another cookie. "Don't worry, dear," he said softly. "You're not in any trouble. It's like our family to want to be bold and explore, right?"

"I guess," I said, watching Poochie grow big on the screen. "I . . . I didn't know what to do yesterday," I said. "I was in a total panic. Poochie grew bigger and bigger and —"

"That growth hormone is one of my *little* experiments," Uncle Victor said. "Yes, I watched the whole thing later when I got home. The looks on your faces made me laugh so hard. But growth hormone is not really what I'm interested in."

He sighed. "What I'm trying to do is much harder than making creatures grow instantly."

I swallowed some of the cookie and wiped my lips with my fingers. "Tell me about your

112

robots," I said. "You said you would tell me everything."

He nodded. The light from the TV monitor flashed on his glasses. I couldn't see his eyes. He leaned forward and tapped his fingers on the table. "Where shall I begin?"

I shrugged. "At the beginning?"

He took a deep breath. He tugged at the sleeves of his lab coat. I could see he was definitely a little nervous about telling me the story.

Finally, he cleared his throat and started: "Kat, I already told you what I've been trying to do here," he said. "I've been building robots and giving them artificial intelligence. My idea is to make them smart enough to survive without human control."

He tapped his fingers on the tabletop again. "As you may know, we scientists create artificial intelligence on computers. We try to copy the way a brain works into a computer program.

"Almost everything a brain can do can be copied into a computer program," he continued. "I worked for many years on such a program. And I was able to make my robots think and talk and understand a lot of things."

He paused. "But then I had a different idea. A crazy idea. But it worked."

I nibbled another cookie. "What was it? What did you do?" I asked.

"I used my *own* brain waves," he answered. "I hooked up my brain to the computer brain. And I copied *my* brain. I made a perfect copy of my brain waves and sent them into the robot brains I was building."

My mouth dropped open. "Wow," I murmured.

I didn't totally understand everything he was telling me. But even I knew this was something amazing.

"And it worked?" I asked. "The robots had your exact brain?"

"Not exactly," he replied. "I couldn't copy everything. And . . . there were some things I didn't think of." He rubbed his chin. "But, yes. I was able to copy my brain waves into the robots."

I gazed at him, waiting for him to continue.

"Well," he started finally, "I guess my success went to my head. I did some bad things, Kat. I did some crazy things I never should have done. And that's when I totally lost control."

28

A silence fell over the narrow room. The monitor screens flashed and flickered. I glanced down at the cookie plate. Without realizing it, I had eaten them all.

My stomach felt heavy. My hands were suddenly ice-cold. I tucked them into my jeans pockets.

"I . . . got carried away," Uncle Victor continued, in a hushed voice. "Since I was using my own brain, I decided to build robots that looked like me. It started out as a joke. I'm not sure why. But it struck me funny.

"I built several robots that looked like me. I gave them my brain. And since I was giving them my brain, I also gave them my *name*. You know me, Kat. It was just my strange sense of humor."

"Well . . . that explains the robot I saw last night," I said. "He told me he was you and —"

"Yes. The robots really *believe* they are me," Uncle Victor said. "And why shouldn't they? They have my brain. But . . . I didn't realize how dangerous it was. I didn't realize how foolish I had been."

I narrowed my eyes at him. "What do you mean?"

"I made them *too* smart," he replied. "I made their brains too much like mine. They decided they didn't need me. They decided they could *be* me. They . . . they . . ."

He began to sputter. He gripped the edge of the table to calm himself.

A chill ran down my back. "What did they do?" I whispered.

"They tried to take over my life, take control of the lab. They tried to imprison me. Lock me up. And take my place."

Another chill swept down my back. "Oh, wow," I murmured. "What did you do?"

"I shut them down, and I locked them up," he replied. "That room at the back of the lab. I closed up all the Victor Frankensteins in there. I locked up all the robots who wanted to take my place. Then I built Frank to keep guard. To keep them in the failure room."

Uncle Victor shook his head. "But . . . they're too smart. They know how to power each other up. They figured out how to escape the failure room. How to escape this house. Some even made

116

it as far as the village. That's why the villagers are afraid of me."

He shuddered. "I have to keep guard at all times. That's why I have Frank. That's why I have the guard dogs. I can't let them capture me and lock me in the failure room. I know that's what they want to do."

"That's horrible," I murmured.

"It's my own fault," he said. "My own fault for making them too smart."

He stared at the monitor in front of him for a while. Then his expression changed, and he turned to me. "Let's talk about something more pleasant," he said. He patted my hand. "Let's talk about my big plans for you."

"For me?" I said. "What kind of plans?"

That strange smile spread over his face again. "Kat, I'm going to turn *you* into a robot."

29

"Excuse me?"

My mouth dropped open. My stomach did a flip-flop.

"Don't be alarmed," Uncle Victor said. "I'm trying to build a female robot. I need to see if there are any problems involved."

"But — but —" I sputtered.

"So I decided to honor you," he said. "Here. Look." He pressed some keys on the keyboard in front of him. A robot appeared on the screen.

"She — she looks just like me!" I cried. "No! You don't plan —"

"You will be the first female," he said. "Kat, don't you want to see what it would be like to have such a close copy of yourself?"

"No," I said. "No way. What if she wants to take over *my* life like your other robots?"

"That won't happen," he replied. "I'll be more careful."

"But, Uncle Victor, I really don't want —"

He raised a hand to silence me. "You can name her. What do you want to name her? How about Kitty? Then we'd have Kitty and Kat!"

"Kill me now," I said. "That's so lame."

"I don't want you to be frightened," Uncle Victor said. "If you are, you will pass the fear onto the robot."

I gasped. "What do you mean? Do you mean you're going to suck out *my* brain?"

"No, no. No way." He patted my hand again. "I'm not sucking out your brain. I'm *copying* it. Copying the brain waves. That's all. It's real easy, Kat. You'll feel a little buzzing in your head. But it isn't painful. It doesn't hurt."

I stared at the robot on the screen. She had my hair. She was dressed in jeans and a maroon sweatshirt. She stood stiffly, eyes shut tight.

"Uncle Victor," I said, "I really don't want to do this. I'm sorry. I don't want to mess up your work. I'd love to help you, but I just can't. I . . . I *won't* let you copy my brain."

"Yes, you will," my uncle replied softly.

"Huh? No. Seriously. I won't —" I insisted.

"Yes," he repeated. "We are going to copy your brain now, Kat. I put something in those cookies, see. You're starting to feel sleepy, right? You're starting to feel very sleepy."

30

I gasped. The room started to fade in and out. I struggled to keep my eyelids open.

My last thought before I fell asleep: *He cannot be my uncle. My uncle Victor would never do this to me.*

Then . . . darkness.

How long was I out cold? I don't know. I awoke, blinking, struggling to focus my eyes.

I saw only a bright light. I felt a hard buzzing in my head.

It took a long time before the light faded and the room came into view. I realized I was seated in Uncle Victor's lab. I saw him hunched over a computer keyboard, typing rapidly.

Then I saw the Kat robot at my side. She had a tall gray cone on her head. The cone was attached to a lot of wires.

And then . . . then . . . I gasped when I saw that the wires were also attached to me. I felt something on my head. Something heavy and tight.

Another gray cone?

The buzzing in my head became a rattle. It made my teeth chatter.

I had to remove the cone.

But my arms . . . they wouldn't move. I gazed down. And saw the black cords tied around my wrists, holding my arms to the arms of the chair.

"Uncle Victor!" I shouted. "Untie me! Untie me — *now*!"

He raised his eyes from the computer monitor. "Sit still, Kat. Don't ruin it. I've just started."

"But, Uncle Victor —"

"You'll be okay," he said, eyes back on the screen. "I'll let you up once the brain wave transfer is made."

"No. No. Please!" I begged.

"We're going to make history, Kat!" he shouted. "History! Don't you want to be famous? The whole world will know about Kitty and Kat!"

He's crazy, I thought. *He can't be my uncle! He CAN'T be!*

I struggled against the cords. But they were too tight to budge.

The rattling buzz shook my head. It felt like someone was drilling on my skull. I shut my eyes, but I couldn't get away from that awful vibrating sound.

"Uncle Victor — PLEASE!" I cried.

I turned when I saw the lab door swing open. Robby stepped in. He saw me seated beside the robot that looked like me. He saw the tall cones on our heads. His eyes went wide with surprise.

"Hey! What's going *on* in here?" he cried.

Uncle Victor waved him in. "Close the door, Robby," he said. "You should see this, too. Kat and I are making history today."

Robby lingered at the door. "I — I don't understand," he stammered. "Why —"

"Just watch closely," my uncle said, tapping on the computer keyboard. "Watch the new robot come to life."

I strained at the cords around my wrists. "Help me, Robby!" I called. "I don't want to do this! Help get me out of this!"

Robby took a few steps toward me. I could see the confusion on his face.

"Don't touch her," Uncle Victor ordered him. "Leave her be. She isn't in any danger."

"But I don't want to *do* this!" I screamed. "He — he's *forcing* me to do this!"

Robby froze. His eyes moved from me to my uncle.

My uncle waved Robby back with one hand. "Just stand there. Wait. It takes only a short while. And it doesn't hurt at all."

"But . . . Kat doesn't want to do it," Robby protested.

"She is just in a panic," Uncle Victor said. "When it is over, she'll be happy. I swear."

The buzzing in my head grew to a roar. It felt as if my head was about to explode.

"Help me!" I screamed. "Robby! Get me *out* of here! Please!"

"Stay there," Uncle Victor warned Robby. "Don't take another step. It's dangerous to stop in the middle."

"I have to untie her," Robby said. His voice trembled. He lurched toward me.

"NO!" Uncle Victor screamed. "You cannot move her while the brain transfer is underway. Stay where you are!"

The sound roared in my head like a jackhammer. I strained at the cords. I tried to kick myself free. "Help me, Robby. Get me out! Hurry!"

I could see the terror on Robby's face as he moved toward me.

"Stop!" Uncle Victor cried. "I'm warning you, Robby. Stop right there!"

Robby was just a few feet away from me when the door at the back of the lab flew open. He stopped and turned at the sound.

A man came bursting out.

He wore a white lab coat. He wore square-framed eyeglasses. He had Uncle Victor's face and wavy brown hair. "Finally! I broke open the lock!" he shouted.

My uncle jumped to his feet. "Get back inside!" he screamed at the new arrival. "Get back inside. I order you!"

But the man didn't move. All three of us froze.

"I'm not going anywhere!" he boomed. "I'm Victor Frankenstein." He turned to me. "I'm your *real* uncle!"

31

"He's a liar!" Uncle Victor stepped away from his computer. His face was red with anger. His eyes bulged. He shook his finger at the intruder. "Liar! Liar!"

"Don't listen to him, Kat," the man from the closet warned. "I built him. Then he locked me up and took over my life. I made him too smart. He's been building robots on his own. An evil army of robots. He's spreading them everywhere."

"Liar!" Uncle Victor screamed, shaking with rage. He turned to me. "I never should have built this copy of myself. He's the most advanced. But he's dangerous. We have to get him into the fail-ure room."

"*You're* the one going in the failure room!" the second Uncle Victor cried, stepping away from the wall. "Back where you belong, once and for all."

I stared from one to the other. I didn't know which one to believe. I wanted to believe the one who had just appeared from behind the door. The first Victor Frankenstein had put me to sleep and was forcing me to share my brain with a robot.

He didn't act like my uncle Victor.

But . . . but . . . They looked so much alike. I didn't know what to think.

"I'm warning you — go back to the failure room! I'm warning you!" Victor One cried. He darted across the lab to Frank. He reached his hand under the arm of the sleeping robot and clicked the power switch.

Frank blinked a few times, then sprung to life. "Frank — grab him! Return him to the failure room! Now!"

Frank nodded, turned, and started to walk stiffly toward Victor Two.

"Don't come any closer, Frank," Victor Two warned. He stiffened, preparing to fight the robot.

Frank stuck out both arms, ready to grab the intruder. Victor One moved across the room to help fight the new arrival.

I motioned to Robby. "Hurry. Over here. Untie me."

Robby dropped beside my chair and worked frantically at the cords that held me down. The two Victors were screaming furiously at each other. I watched Frank step up to Victor Two.

Robby tugged the cords away, and I jumped to my feet. My heart was pounding. My head spun as I glanced from one Victor to the other.

Which is my real uncle?

I gasped as Frank wrapped his hands around Victor Two's waist — and hoisted him off the ground. Victor Two squirmed and twisted, and swung both hands wildly. But Frank was too strong for him.

"Yes!" Victor One pumped a fist in the air. "Dump him in the failure room, Frank!" He turned to me. He blinked when he saw I was standing up. "Don't be afraid, Kat," he said. "This will all be over in a second."

Don't be afraid? I thought. *You tied me to a chair and tried to drain my brain. Of COURSE I'm afraid!*

Frank held Victor Two in his powerful grasp and began to march toward the door on the back wall. Victor Two slumped in defeat. He uttered a sigh.

And then he reached out both hands and grabbed Frank's head by the sides. He twisted the robot's head with a quick hard motion — and ripped it off Frank's body.

A high, shrill squeal escaped the headless robot.

Victor Two heaved Frank's head against the wall. It made a shattering sound and bounced across the floor. Frank's body slumped lifelessly in place.

Victor Two stepped away easily. He turned and came toward Victor One. His face twisted in fury. His hands were balled into tight fists.

Victor One turned to Robby and me. "Help me!" he cried. "Don't let him get away with this. You have to believe me. He's an evil robot."

"I'm your uncle," Victor Two cried. "I'm no robot. Step back. The two of you — step back. I built this robot, and now I'm going to destroy him."

Which one? Which one?

How could I tell?

Suddenly, as they prepared to fight, I had an idea.

32

I saw Poochie standing at the door to the lab. The little dog peered into the room, his head lowered as if frightened by all the shouting.

I hurried over to him and lifted him into my arms. His little heart was pounding hard. I carried him to the center of the room.

The two Victors were still shouting at each other, circling each other, preparing to fight.

Robby turned to me. "What are you doing with the dog?"

"Poochie knows his real master," I said. "The dog knows who is human and who is a robot. He'll show us which one is my uncle."

Robby shrugged. "It's worth a try."

I set Poochie down gently on the floor. "Go ahead, boy. Go to him. Go to the real Uncle Victor. Go!" I gave him a push toward the two Victors.

Robby and I stood tensely, watching as the little dog padded across the floor. He ran straight to Victor One. He began tugging on Victor One's pants leg.

"See? He wants to play with his real master," I said. "Poochie just showed us who the real Uncle Victor is!"

"Now you know I spoke the truth!" Victor One cried. "Hurry. Help me get this faulty robot locked up safely in the failure room."

Poochie tugged at his pants leg. Victor One grabbed the other Victor by the shoulders.

"Kat, you're making a big mistake!" Victor Two cried.

"No, I'm not. Poochie knows his real master!" I said. "I'm not confused anymore."

Robby and I grabbed the Victor robot. He kicked and thrashed. But the three of us overpowered him and pushed him into the back room. Uncle Victor latched the door carefully after him.

Then he made his way over to the wall and bent to examine Frank's head. The head was lying faceup on the floor. Victor lifted it carefully and turned it around in his hands.

Poochie continued to tug at his pants leg. Victor gave the dog a gentle shove, trying to remove him. "Not now, boy," he said. "We can't play now. Not now."

"Oh, NOOOO!"

I let out a cry as I realized what Poochie was doing. The dog tugged Victor's pants leg up — and I saw the power switch on Victor's ankle.

I grabbed Robby by the shoulder. "Look! Oh, wow. We got it wrong! Robby, we got it wrong!"

We both quickly realized that Poochie hadn't shown us the real Victor. He wanted to show us which one was the *robot*!

Victor gave Poochie a hard kick, sending the little dog sliding across the floor.

"We locked up the wrong Victor!" I cried. "We know you're the robot!"

He turned with a scowl on his face — and *heaved* Frank's head at me. I ducked and it flew into the wall.

"Maybe you *did* lock up the wrong one, Kat dear," he sneered. "What are you going to do about it?"

He moved quickly toward us. "I *know* what you're going to do. You're going to get back in that chair so I can finish transferring your brain. After today, you won't be needing it anymore."

33

Robby and I didn't wait. We didn't have to say a word to each other.

I leaped high and tackled the Victor robot around the neck. Robby tackled him around the waist.

He dropped hard to the floor. Before he could put up a struggle, I reached for his ankle — and clicked *off* the power switch.

The Victor robot uttered a groan. His eyes rolled up in his head. He didn't move.

Struggling to catch my breath, I ran to the door against the back wall. Robby hurried close behind me.

"My poor uncle," I said breathlessly. "How long has he been trapped back here?"

I unlatched the door and tugged it open.

"Oh, wow." In the dim light, I saw faces staring back at me. They all looked like Uncle Victor. Packed into the little room were at least a dozen Victors, all in long white lab coats.

My eyes moved frantically from one to the other.

"Which one of you . . . ?" I cried in a trembling voice. "Which one of you is my real uncle Victor?" I choked out.

"I am!" the one closest to me shouted.

"I am!" said the one next to him.

"I am!" came a shout from the back.

"I am!"

"I am!" "I am!" "I am!" "I am! I am! I am! I am!"

34

"No!" I cried. "No! This can't be!"

I stumbled back. I had to get out of that room.

"I am!" "I am!" "I am!" The shouts continued until the voices made my head throb.

I let out a gasp as I bumped into someone behind me. Robby? No. Robby stood by the door.

I spun around — and stared at a man in a black suit, a white shirt, and a red-and-black-striped tie. He carried a brown briefcase in one hand and a large suitcase in the other.

He squinted at me. "Kat? What are you *doing* here?" he said.

My mouth dropped open. "Uncle Victor?"

He nodded. He moved quickly to the door and slammed it shut. As he latched it, the cries from the other side faded.

"Kat, I've been in France," he said. "I was expecting you *next* week."

"N-no," I stammered. "I arrived on Friday. You said —"

He dropped the two cases and slapped his forehead. "Oh, no. I don't believe it. I could *swear* I wrote you down for next week. Oh, my goodness. Why can't I ever keep any dates straight?"

He rushed forward and wrapped me in a hug. "I'm so sorry. So sorry I wasn't here to greet you. I hurried back here to get ready for you. I wanted everything to be nice when you arrived."

"I . . . I . . ." I was so happy to see him, I was speechless.

Poochie yapped and jumped up on his legs. Uncle Victor bent and lifted the dog high. Whimpering with happiness, Poochie licked his face.

"Stop! Stop!" Uncle Victor cried, lowering the dog. He laughed. "You know how ticklish I am."

I had to ask. "Uncle Victor? Can robots be ticklish?"

"Of course not," he said. "They're machines." He glanced at the door. "Hey, I hope those robots didn't give you any trouble. They can be a real pain."

"Well . . ." I started.

But I didn't get any further, because four yapping white dogs came trotting into the lab. "Whoa!" I cried. "They all look like Poochie!"

"Of course they do," Uncle Victor said. "They're clones. They're all clones of Poochie. I took them to Paris to show them off. Aren't they wonderful?"

The five Poochies barked and jumped gleefully on my uncle and me.

"I'm finished with robots," Uncle Victor said. "I can't get them to work properly. That's why I locked them away. Now I spend all my time cloning. I can't wait to tell you about it, Kat."

"Cool," I said. I could barely hear him over the yapping dogs.

Uncle Victor grabbed my arm. "Hey, I have a *great* idea. Why don't I clone you? Would you like that, Kat? Would you like a clone of yourself to keep you company?"

I pulled my arm free and frowned at him. "You're joking, right?" I said. "That's your crazy sense of humor, right? Uncle Victor — please . . . Tell me that you're joking."

He rubbed his hands together. "Why not *four* of you? How about it, dear? *Four* Kats. Or maybe ten? You could rule the world! How about it?"

Then we both burst out laughing.

Goosebumps®

MOST WANTED

The list continues with book #5

DR. MANIAC WILL
SEE YOU NOW

Here's a sneak peek!

5

I stepped into the wide front entryway to the museum. The ceiling was a mile high, lined with tall windows. A huge red-and-blue chandelier hung down over the long front desk.

My shoes clicked on the white marble floor. The sound echoed through the huge room. My eyes swept over the big posters of superheroes that covered the walls.

"Hey, Kahuna. How's it going?" I shouted.

Behind the desk, Kahuna looked up from the graphic novel he was reading. "Yo, Richard. Keeping it real?"

Big Kahuna is the main greeter and curator of the museum. I don't know his real name. I call him Kahuna. We're like friends. I mean, I spend more time with him than with my own family.

Kahuna has a long, serious face. He wears black-framed glasses. He has dark brown hair pulled back in a ponytail. Dangling from one ear, he has a big silver pirate hoop earring. And he has colorful tattoos of his favorite superheroes up and down his arms and across his chest. He wears sleeveless T-shirts to show them off.

He's a cool guy, but I've never seen him smile.

I stepped up to the desk. "Shazam, bro," he said. We bumped knuckles. "Where have you been lately?"

I spun around and sneezed. I held my breath and made sure I wasn't going to sneeze again. Then I turned back to him. "Just been to the allergy doctor," I said. "He gave me a shot."

Kahuna snickered. "I don't think it's working." He pulled open a drawer under the desk and reached inside. "Got something for you."

He pulled out two comic books. I couldn't see the covers, but they looked pretty old. The paper was yellow.

Kahuna is the greatest dude ever. He always finds comics he knows I'll like. And he pretty much lets me do whatever I want in the museum. I can go into any of the rare comics rooms and spend as much time as I want looking at the old collections.

He raised the comics for me to see. On the covers, I saw a chimpanzee with a black mask pulled down over his head. "The Masked Monkey!" I cried.

Kahuna nodded. "These are very rare, bro. The only two *Masked Monkey* comics ever produced. From 1973. You seen them before? *Of course* you haven't." He answered his own question.

My hands shook a little as I took the two comics from him. These were very rare and valuable. "Awesome," I said. "Totally awesome. I'll take them to the Reading Room and read them. Thanks, Kahuna."

We bumped knuckles again. Then I carefully gripped the comics in front of me as I made my way to the Reading Room at the back of the long front hall.

My shoes clicked on the marble floor. I hurried past the bronze statues of the Martian Mayhem and his archenemy, Plutopus.

Some days I stopped to look at the hundreds of framed comic book covers that spread over one entire wall. But not today. I was too eager to study these valuable *Masked Monkey* comics.

I didn't see anyone else in the museum. Why wasn't it more popular? Didn't people realize this was the best comic book museum in the *world*?

I passed the video projection room and the tall statue of Captain Protoplasm. The auditorium stood dark and silent.

I trotted to the end of the hall. I knew I didn't have much time. My parents were probably at home now, arguing over what we should have for dinner.

"Oh, wow." I let out a cry when I saw the Reading Room doors were closed. I grabbed the knob and turned it. "No. Please."

The doors were locked.

I turned and started back to the front to get the key from Kahuna. As I walked, I carefully wiped my hands on the legs of my jeans. I didn't want to get sweat on the valuable comics.

I was halfway to the front desk when I heard shouts. I heard a crash. Then a dull *thud*. Another shout.

Was Kahuna fighting with someone?

I took off, running to the desk. My shoes skidded on the slick floor. My heart started to pound.

The desk came into view. But — whoa. Where was Kahuna?

He wasn't in his usual place, sitting on the tall stool behind the desk.

I skidded to a stop. I stared at the stranger behind the desk. I couldn't see his face. He had his back turned.

I tucked the *Masked Monkey* comics into my backpack and stepped up to the desk. "Hey, where's Kahuna?" I asked. My voice came out high and shrill.

"He had to leave," the man replied. He didn't turn around.

I blinked. Something weird. The man was standing in the tall trash can behind the desk.

I stared at his back. He wore a long black trench coat. He had silver hair falling down over the collar.

Slowly, he turned to face me — and I let out a startled gasp.

His eyes — they had no pupils. They were solid white.

"Can I help you?" he asked.

I stared into those blank white eyes. No pupils. No pupils at all. Was he blind?

"Can I help you?" he repeated. His voice was scratchy and hoarse. His head was bald and shiny and shaped like a lightbulb.

"Uh . . . no," I said. "I mean . . ."

He picked up a pencil and scribbled some words on the desk pad.

He's not blind. But he has no pupils.

"I'm . . . uh . . . late for dinner," I stammered. "I'll come back when Kahuna is here."

He nodded. "Have a *super* evening," he said. But he said it coldly. Like a threat.

A chill of fear made me shudder. What was this about? I knew I'd heard a shout and then a crash. And then suddenly, this weird dude stood behind Kahuna's desk.

"Bye," I said. I spun away from the desk and ran out of the museum.

I didn't realize I'd taken the *Masked Monkey* comics home with me until after dinner.

We had a typical dinner at the Dreezer house. Mom and Dad argued about whether the short ribs were tender enough. Ernie was clowning around and acting like a jerk, pretending he was a string puppet. And he spilled his apple juice. But they didn't shout at him or anything because everything he does is adorable.

I dropped a carrot on the floor, and Mom and Dad started shouting about what a clumsy klutz I am. Then I sneezed on my dinner plate, and they told me to leave the table.

Typical.

Up in my room, I started to unload my backpack — and there they were. The two rare comic books.

I knew I had to return them to the museum tomorrow. Kahuna would understand that I didn't mean to take them.

I carefully spread the comics on my desk and began to read the first one.

Even though the hero was a monkey, the art was very realistic. The intro said that no one knew the origin of the Masked Monkey. His power is in his mask. He may be a chimp, but he has the strength of *ten gorillas*.

"That's a mean monkey!" I murmured to myself.

Downstairs, I heard my parents arguing over the best way to load the dishwasher. And then I heard another, closer sound. The thud of running footsteps.

I spun around as Ernie came bursting into my room. He let out a cry and ran straight to my desk.

"Stop!" I cried. I tried to shove him away.

Too late. He grabbed the two comics and took off with them.

The little thief is always taking my things. But this time he'd gone too far.

I jumped to my feet. "Give those back!" I shouted. "Now! I'm not going to play around with you!"

He stopped in the hall and stuck his tongue out at me.

I took a few steps toward him. I kept my eyes on the comics. I was trembling, so angry I thought I could explode.

"Those are valuable," I said. "They belong to the museum. They are very rare. Give them back to me."

Ernie shook his head. He had a sick grin on his weasel face. "They're mine now," he said.

"GIVE THEM BACK!" I shrieked.

About the Author

R.L. Stine's books are read all over the world. So far, his books have sold more than 300 million copies, making him one of the most popular children's authors in history. Besides Goosebumps, R.L. Stine has written the teen series Fear Street and the funny series Rotten School, as well as the Mostly Ghostly series, The Nightmare Room series, and the two-book thriller *Dangerous Girls*. R.L. Stine lives in New York with his wife, Jane, and Minnie, his King Charles spaniel. You can learn more about him at www.RLStine.com.

NEED MORE THRILLS?

GET Goosebumps!

WATCH

ON TV

ONLY ON

hub

ON DVD

PLAY

Wii

LISTEN

◢◣SCHOLASTIC
www.scholastic.com/goosebumps

THERE'S ALWAYS ROOM FOR ONE MORE SCREAM!

An all-new series from fright-master R.L. Stine!

The Original Bone-Chilling Series

—with Exclusive Author Interviews!

R. L. Stine's Fright Fest!
Now with Splat Stats and More!

THE SCARIEST PLACE ON EARTH!

Goosebumps HorrorLand

HELP! WE HAVE STRANGE POWERS!
R.L. STINE

Goosebumps HorrorLand

ESCAPE FROM HORRORLAND
R.L. STINE

Goosebumps HorrorLand

THE STREETS OF PANIC PARK
R.L. STINE

Goosebumps HorrorLand

WHEN THE GHOST DOG HOWLS
R.L. STINE

Goosebumps HorrorLand

LITTLE SHOP OF HAMSTERS
R.L. STINE

Goosebumps HorrorLand

HEADS, YOU LOSE!
R.L. STINE

Goosebumps HorrorLand

WEIRDO HALLOWEEN
R.L. STINE

Goosebumps HorrorLand

THE WIZARD OF OOZE
R.L. STINE

Goosebumps HorrorLand

SLAPPY NEW YEAR!
R.L. STINE

Goosebumps HorrorLand

THE HORROR AT CHILLER HOUSE
R.L. STINE

Catch the
MOST WANTED
Goosebumps® villains
UNDEAD OR ALIVE!